WHAT ELSE IS A HEART FOR?

The quotation in "A Few Accidents Among Friends" is from "Pas des Deux" © 1984 Susan Thornton and appeared in *The Seattle Review*. Dayv James-French wishes to thank the Ontario Arts Council and the Regional Municipality of Ottawa-Carleton. "Heaven Full of Astronauts" is © 1987 *The Antioch Review.*

WHAT ELSE IS A HEART FOR?

BY DAYV JAMES-FRENCH

Porcepic Books
an imprint of

Beach Holme Publishing
Vancouver

First Edition

This book is published by Beach Holme Publishing, #226—2040 West 12th Ave., Vancouver, BC, V6J 2G2. This is a Porcepic Book.

We acknowledge the generous assistance of The Canada Council and the BC Ministry of Small Business, Tourism and Culture.

THE CANADA COUNCIL FOR THE ARTS SINCE 1957 | LE CONSEIL DES ARTS DU CANADA DEPUIS 1957

Editor: Joy Gugeler
Production and Design: Teresa Bubela

Cover Art: *Midnight Men* by Joan Krawczyk, 1986, acrylic on canvas, 152.4 cm x 243.84 cm. Collection of Dr. Miles Cohen. Reprinted with permission of the artist and owner.

Canadian Cataloguing in Publication Data:

James-French, Dayv
What else is a heart for?

(A Porcepic Book)
ISBN 0-88878-382-5

I. Title. II. Series.

PS8569.A463W53 1998 C813'.54 C98-900288-8
PR9199.3.J35W53 1998

CONTENTS

One does not ask, skating on a pond, how the dark sky carries its burden of starlight. I don't, in any case.
— John Cheever

I try to believe...But I can't.
Need is not quite belief.
— Anne Sexton

CERVINE

In the kitchen, Joshua is talking to the chicken parts. From the living room, Dan can't help hearing, although he's listening against his will. With the pump in the backyard turned off, the house seems overly quiet. The pool hasn't been entirely drained—there's about four feet of water in the sloping deep end—but Dan doesn't want to antagonize the neighbours with the noise at dinnertime. He might even leave the rest until Monday, not to disturb their weekend quiet; he may need their good favour later. He has no idea what's involved in replacing a pool liner. At the very least, he assumes a dumpster will be parked on the street outside, narrowing the passage to the end of the crescent.

"I'm sorry you were de-beaked as a chick," Joshua is saying. He's fourteen years old and, Dan thinks, very young for his age. His voice still has a child's tonelessness, high-pitched and invariable. "You shouldn't have had to live in a wire cage. But now you're going to be dinner and I want you to know your whole life wasn't wasted."

Dan snaps back the first page of the newspaper. Last night it was hamburger. Steroids in the grain or something. He glances at a headline, registering only the word *Ethiopia,* and gives up. He folds the paper and drops it on the coffee table, waiting for Laurie to finish. They take turns starting with the front or back, exchanging sections, reading towards the middle. The rotation was her idea and, since she had been married before, he assumed its merits. In his heart, he admired his own commitment to that unequivocal strength of *compromise.* On Thursdays he stares blindly at Fashion for as long as twenty minutes, waiting for her to pass over Local. Sometimes he has a drink. When he does, he always asks if she wants a glass of wine, while he's up.

"Does he *have* to do that?"

"What?" Laurie looks up from the Business pages.

"Talk to the food."

"It's only the meat," she says. Her eyes drop back to the page. "I wonder if we shouldn't have gotten that airline stock?"

"But *why?"*

"Well, it says here they're getting those new Airbuses. If they're really more fuel efficient, that might reduce expenses and increase profits, even after the cost of the planes. Of course, now that the story's in the paper, I'm sure the stock's jumped up."

"Let's forget the Airbus. Why does he talk to the meat?"

"He's very sensitive about animals being exploited. His father's the same way. It makes him feel better about eating meat if he doesn't pretend it's from the supermarket."

"It *is* from the supermarket."

"I mean, originally. *He* means, I should say. I really don't think about it one way or the other." Laurie stands, handing him the paper. "Section? I'm going to get a glass of wine. Do you want a drink?"

"Please." Dan takes the paper. He's never met Jack, Laurie's first husband, and he wonders, again, why Laurie gave him custody of Joshua. He imagines a morning when she put breakfast on the table then quietly left the room, going upstairs to call a cab and pack an overnight bag. He can see her slip down the stairs and out the door, closing it quietly behind her. All the while Jack and Joshua were apologizing to the bacon. Maybe the eggs as well. Dan's sure he'll find out before the summer's over. Joshua is here until the middle of August; it's the second week of July.

"Pasta or rice with the chicken?" Laurie asks, holding out his drink.

"Pasta." He watches her go back to the kitchen, hears her tell Joshua, "Noodles." He looks down at an artist's conception of an Airbus. After a moment, he thinks, What about their *shoes?*

The pool water has found a slight dip in the lawn and the back yard looks like a lake. No, a rice paddy. Clumps of very green grass stick out of a silver plain. So far, the basement hasn't been flooded. Dan can't decide if he should pump out the rest of the pool and have whatever happens happen all at once, or wait to see if evaporation and seepage will level things off before he adds the rest of the water. He has the pump until noon Monday. It's a bright yellow machine, the size of a small tractor. His car needed a trailer hitch, which he bought, and a flatbed, rented, to get it home. The flatbed is pulled up beside the garage, in the strip of lawn between it and the next house. Laurie and Joshua have taken the car to the mall.

"He needs a haircut," Laurie said that morning. "He's not in Edmonton now. And I want to get him some shirts and shorts that look *summery.* It would seem his father is incapable of buying anything that's not blue. He dresses Joshua like, I don't know, like an *accountant* or something."

Dan was standing at the door to the master bathroom, wearing a terry robe over the Y-fronts he'd slept in, in case he had to get up in the night. After some searching before bedtime, he'd been forced to accept that the pyjamas he'd once owned now existed only in his memory; they weren't in the house. Laurie was looking at him as if he was supposed to respond to what she said.

"Huhm," he nodded. He didn't know what to say. The boy did look a bit...serious. But it wasn't just his clothes. A couple of times Dan had been surprised to realize the two of them had been in the same room for a while, unaware of each other. Dan would look up and, startled by the boy's presence, try to recover with an off-hand, "How's it going, sport?" while feeling his mouth slide into a slick grin. Joshua would nod and say, "Fine." They'd blink at each other for a few moments until Laurie came into the room, or else, by an odd, mutual timing, they'd turn back to whatever they'd been doing. Dan has no idea what these intervals mean, but they leave him feeling isolated and helpless.

Laurie was still speaking, a blur of vowels around the brush of her lip gloss.

He said, “Huhm,” again.

“And I guess we’ll grab a bite there. The yogurt place, probably.” Laurie patted his chest as she passed him, leaving the bathroom free. “Haircut, clothes, lunch.” She punctuated the list by dropping her wallet and keys into her purse, snapping it shut. “That’s a full morning for us. You can find something for yourself?”

“Sure thing,” Dan said. “I’ll be fine. You guys go nuts.”

Now he’s wading through the yard in a pair of olive and yellow rubbers that the clerk at the hardware store called “gum tuckies.” He’s not wearing socks and the touch of the boot tops against his shins makes his legs feel naked. His legs *are* naked; his nylon shorts don’t come down much lower than his crotch, and they’re split up the sides. When he was getting dressed, he must have thought he’d end up doing some swimming.

The sodden ground makes a wet, satisfying sound under his feet. Impulsively, Dan stamps down hard. The water rises up like the walls of a volcano, slurps over, and settles. Dan stamps again, harder. In seconds, he’s jumping on the spot, like he’s skipping rope. Both feet: three, four, shift, left foot, five, six. He hits the ground with enough impact to splash water higher than his waist. Higher than his head, even. His face feels wet. By the time he’s able to force himself to stop, he’s as damp as if he’d just showered. His breathing is audibly arythmic.

"Woosh." He exhales as much as he can, then sucks in air with small, hiccupping noises until his lungs are full. *"Heh. Heh. Heh."*

"This is hard work, this pool?"

Dan turns around so quickly that water droplets spin off his hair.

"Oh, Deepak. Hi." The Sahasrabudis are relatively new neighbours. They live three houses down, around the corner. Because of the curve of the street, the end of their backyard defines the side of his own, the meeting marked by a five foot chain link fence. Beyond that, past a lower, lattice-weave fence, is the Airport Parkway, a double line of asphalt cutting through a small forest.

"Hard work?" he repeats. "No, I was just, uh, warming up. I'm not sure how much I'm going to get done today."

"That will be a very nice thing to have when the hot weather arrives."

"I guess so. I'm not sure it's nice enough to justify having it here the other ten months of the year."

"A question of balance." Deepak nods wisely. "This is true of many things. But it sits there, whether you use it or not. And when you want the pleasure, it is available to you."

"That's one way of looking at it, I guess. But there's this constant maintenance. Like over there—at the very back?—the fence boards need to be replaced. Maybe you can't see from here, the spirea has it covered, but you could knock the whole thing down with one swift kick."

"You would do this?"

"That's not really the point. What I mean is, to have the

pool I have to keep the fence in good repair. You know, for the insurance. A pool's what they call 'an attractive nuisance'."

"Ah." Deepak nods again. "And what is that?"

"Well, let's see..." Dan looks around the yard, as if he expected another example to be revealed to him. "Attractive. A child could see the pool and want to go swimming, but if no one's watching, he could drown. So the onus is on me to make sure he, or she, can't get near it in the first place. I'm responsible for the fact that it looks like fun, but can be dangerous."

Deepak's hands are folded together in front of his mouth. His eyes are open very wide. He moves his head back and forth and makes a sound somewhere between a pant and a sigh. Dan wonders if the man has had too much sun. After a moment he realizes what he's hearing is laughter.

"It is a wife that you mean," Deepak says. Then he pants and sighs a little more.

"I'm sorry?" Dan strains for a connection between that and what he's said.

"She looks like fun, but she's dangerous. An attractive nuisance."

"Really, Deepak. I don't think we say things like that any more."

"But this is funny. I am thinking I could send it to the *Playboy's* "Party Jokes." For their *Our Unabashed Dictionary.* You are aware of the magazine of that name?"

"Playboy? Sure, I've read it. God, it's been a while, though. The last issue I bought," Dan pauses, amazed to

have such a detail available in his memory, "was with Joan Baez."

"That one I have not seen." Deepak looks over his shoulder at his house, a furtive twist of his neck. "A real babe?"

"She was the interview," Dan explains. "It was ten or twelve years ago. Fifteen. When I was in my teens. I haven't looked at the magazine since." His neighbour looks disappointed, and Dan can't think of anything to say. He starts backing up, making vague comments about changing into dry clothes, although his shorts are no longer plastered to him. There's an odour rising from his skin, a dank, foresty smell.

"See you later," he concludes, turning to walk towards his house in a determined manner.

Inside, he stands under the shower, humming, "There But For Fortune," one hand on the tap to slowly cool down the water. He hopes he's not remembering this accurately: it was almost *twenty-five* years ago that he read the Joan Baez interview. The centrefold's name was Janice Pennington. She wanted to be an actress. She'd be almost fifty now. He's never seen her in a movie or on television. Not that he can recall. Of course, he doesn't know anyone who's living a life mapped out in August, 1969. Dan was fifteen that summer, less than a year older than Joshua is now. He wonders if the boy knows *everything,* the way Dan did. The only thing he hadn't known was that everything gets more and more complex.

Laurie is furious. Dan could tell even before she came into the house. He heard the choked-off rip of the emergency brake only seconds before the side door slammed and Joshua disappeared up the stairs, a flash of blue, a swirl of multi-coloured shopping bags. In the time it took Dan to reach the kitchen, Laurie was coming in with the groceries. Her face was set in a tight mask, all business.

"Here, let me," Dan says, reaching for one of the brown paper sacks.

"I've got them all balanced," Laurie says. "Could you wait until I put them *down.*" She has to lift herself onto the balls of her feet to get the bags unto the counter. "There. *Now* you can deal with them. Thank you."

"I've got it." Dan looks into one bag, lifts out a small tin of tomato paste. He reaches under a loaf of sandwich bread, feeling for more cans. He has a system: tins and dry goods stay on the counter until only meat and vegetables are left in the bags, which get put directly into the refrigerator's crisper drawers. Ambiguous items, like pickles and mustard, require a second opinion. The routine makes him careless and he asks, over his shoulder. "So, how'd it go?"

"I don't want to talk about it. I just want to sit here and calm down enough until I can think rationally and then decide if I should kill him or not. I would *like* to smoke a cigarette, but I don't think killing *myself* would be productive."

"Okay." Dan turns around, making a T with his hands. "A little time out." She doesn't smile. "Hey, I made coffee. Want some?"

"I'm already like *this.*" Laurie holds out her own hands.

Her spread-out fingers vibrate with tension.

"No coffee."

"Even his father must have told him there's a difference between questioning authority in a productive manner, and wasting your time with stupid, juvenile challenges. He knew I'd be upset, you can count on that. Being hurtful, that's all he's doing. I should have caught on when he told me I didn't have to wait for him at the barber's."

"Ah. He didn't get his hair cut?"

"He got his hair cut all right."

"Just a little off the ends?" That's what Dan would tell the barber when his parents dragged him to one after the school sent him home with a note threatening suspension. "Do you want me to talk to him?"

"What would you say? 'Go back there and get your hair'?"

"It's too short?"

"In places."

"Well, that doesn't sound so bad. I mean, hair grows."

"It's not the hair. It's, I don't know, the attitude. Like he was scheming to get it done behind my back. If he'd just come to me and asked, 'Can I do something that'll give Dad a heart attack?' I would have said—" Laurie makes a strangled noise and opens her purse to get a tissue. "I would have said, 'You know your father doesn't *have* a heart, only a social conscience.'" She blows her nose, shaking her head with the effort. "It galls me to think that I was pushing a cart up and down the grocery store aisles, planning menus and feeling over-dressed, and wondering, once the pool is working, who we know with kids his age to have over for a barbecue and stuff, and all the while he was getting clipped like some kind of overbred *dog.*" She tries to laugh, then blows her nose again.

"You're upset with him." Dan folds one of the bags into thirds, slowly, then smooths it flat. "That's understandable. But it's not like getting his ear pierced, is it? Or a tattoo?"

"A *tattoo?* What are you talking about?"

"This is pretty small stuff, isn't it? In the big picture."

"I can't help how I feel."

"Of course not." Dan kneels in front of the refrigerator with the last of the groceries. Mushrooms on the left, styrofoam tray of veal cutlets on the right. *Veal?* He slides the drawers closed, then presses his forehead against the edge of the cold metal shelf.

Behind him, Laurie says, "I am *not* a senile fossil."

Not quite human-looking, is what Dan thinks.

Joshua is wearing an athletic top like an undershirt, but banana yellow and deeply scooped at the neck and under the arms. Where his skin shows, it isn't much more than a beige film over his bones. He's standing at the kitchen door, not quite leaning against the wall behind him, although his upper body slants back as though he's been arrested in the act of entering the room. Neon-green Spandex bicycle shorts girdle his body from waist to knees. Dan winces at the flatness of the crotch, looks down at the unlaced high-top sneakers, as incongruously huge as the paws on a puppy of mixed pedigree.

"What's upset your mother," he starts, trying to formulate

a line of logic, some way to suggest that Laurie might have a point about Joshua looking weird, and then he realizes that Joshua's clothes are not the issue. Laurie must have picked them out, possibly after she made Joshua try them on. Dan tries to take in the hair without obviously staring; it's a modified brushcut, with a short pigtail on one side at the back, a tuft rising over the forehead. The rest of his scalp is bushy as a hamster. Two snips with a scissors would bring everything into line. But, Dan thinks, *why bother?* If Joshua is going to dress like an android, there's no point in looking like a person from the neck up.

Joshua is looking at something slightly above and beyond Dan's right shoulder, through the aluminum screen door, into the yard. He's probably embarrassed, having a stranger witness his being an object of maternal disapproval. He might even be thinking of Dan as another guy, and be suffering some reduction in status. It's an oddly endearing thought, flattering, and Dan claps his palms together as though something has been settled, to indicate he's not going to finish whatever speech he'd started.

In front of him, Joshua snaps his arms up, like he's reaching for a long pass, or shielding his eyes from bright headlights on a dark road. His skin loses its colour, fading from beige to pale grey to white. The tips of his ears turn pink, then red. He makes a noise in his throat, a noise that sounds like *moof, moof.*

He's having a heart attack? Dan thinks, his own heart suspending itself between beats. Sweet Christ, a *stroke?*

There's an odd rustling all of a sudden, an artificial

sound, as though someone in special-effects were crunching potato chips against a microphone to suggest the crackling of a forest fire. The sound seems to be coming from all four corners of the room. Nausea, second-hand, rises in Dan's throat; he is scared in a way he's never been frightened before. There's no senses but fear. A low, low note—operatic in its physicality—thrubs through the air, through Dan's head, entering each ear and somehow cancelled out in the middle of his brain. From temple to temple, he's an empty space; the eye of a hurricane, a gaping fissure in the earth's crust. Whatever is dangerous is external. With no room for thought, purely by instinct, he steps back, one hand swinging wildly behind him for the crash bar on the screen door. At the moment he feels it give, he reaches out and pulls Joshua towards him and rolls the two of them into the pale yellow evening outside. A second later—less than a second, he shouts, "Out! *Laurie,* get out of the *house!"*

Joshua twists away from Dan and yells, "Mom!" He's short of breath—Dan may have been squeezing his arms—but he recovers a nearly normal tone to say, "Don't yank me *around,"* and he smacks the back of his hand against Dan's upper arm before taking four or five fast steps to the edge of the deck. Again, he yells, "Mom!"

"Sweet—" Dan's urgency evaporates at the moment he hears Joshua's voice. It's quiet again. There wasn't an earthquake (he realizes that had been his concern). The house will not fall in on itself. Laurie is safe. Where he was fearful, now he feels glassy and hollow, fragile still. He's confused. "What was that all about?"

"I tried to tell you." Joshua calls out another, impatient, "Mom!" He turns and points at the pool "It's a moose."

Mossy antlers large as whale bones; dark brown fur, short as a cow's, but seemingly acres of it; a great dewlap under its neck like a woolly mailpouch. Dan can't take it all in. The animal dominates the pool the way a car takes up most of the space in a garage. The moose's hind hooves are flat on the bottom of the deep end. Through the water, rippling with shallow crests and troughs, the globes of the knee-joints seems to shrink and swell. Its shorter forelegs are braced on the slope of the pool. In the huge head with its fleshy over-lip, whiteless eyes the size of grapefruit look comparatively tiny and somehow blind, stupidly expressionless.

Joshua is moving back and forth without taking his eyes off the moose, keeping a safe distance from the edge of the pool, about three or four feet. His mouth works furiously and, when he speaks, finally, it's in a whisper.

"He walked through that fence like it was only *feathers* or something."

"Look at the size of it," Dan says, agreeing, also in a whisper. Laurie shouts something from the house. He steps closer to the boy, so his bicep is level with Joshua's shoulder, the two of them facing the pool. There's a pleasant, loamy scent in the air, nothing at all like a wet dog.

The moose turns its head towards them, making moist, snuffling noises. Laurie shouts again.

"He could've come right in the house." Joshua sounds like this would have been a splendid thing to have happen;

there's a deep satisfaction in his voice. "Come in right through the *wall.*"

"While we were at the table?" Dan suggests. He puts on a not-very-good British accent, to sound refined. "'We have company. Do set another place for the moose.' Then we'd be sitting in a cloud of plaster dust, with bricks dropping on the floor, and a huge great space open to the outside. Do you think he'd want a cutlet?"

"Naw," Joshua shakes his head. "Moose aren't *carnivores.* He might have some vegetables though."

"Like what, a truckload of salad?"

Laurie calls to them from the deck. "Will you get over here?"

"We'll come back." Dan looks right into Joshua's eyes for a moment, before they cross the lawn, squishing through the puddles of water.

"I was calling you," she says as they approach.

"I called *you*, before," Joshua says. "Why didn't you come see?"

"I can see enough from here. Josh, I don't think you should get so close. That thing is probably covered with fleas, and I don't know what else."

"I didn't *touch* it." Joshua turns to face the pool again. There's a change in his expression when he looks at the animal; he radiates an awed, enviable serenity.

"We were back a ways," Dan says. "It looks pretty harmless. Enormous and remarkable, to be sure, but it doesn't seem dangerous." He laughs. Laurie narrows her eyes at him, over Joshua's head, and he adds, "I mean, it's not about to get out and charge or anything." As he says this, the truth of the statement occurs to him.

"My god, we have a *moose* trapped in our swimming pool."

From the bedroom window, in the warm glow of the bug light over the back door, Dan can make out the pale grey gleam of the duvet spread over the grass. After some careful checking, Laurie decided there was a patch of lawn dry enough for Joshua to camp out on, so he could keep an eye on the moose. He trekked out in his pyjamas with a flashlight and the *M* volume of the encyclopedia, looking like a precocious archaeologist. Dan can't see a separate ring of illumination on the bedding; it's possible the boy is already asleep. He pulls the curtain closed and starts unbuttoning his shirt.

"I think that went okay," he says, sitting on the edge of the bed to take off his socks. "With the Sahasrubudis and all."

"Saruda seemed nice," Laurie agrees. "Even when I couldn't keep a straight face, hearing her name. Saruda Sahasrabudi sounds like you're trying to say something with a mouthful of peanut butter."

"What about Deepak?"

"Well, it's not *John,* I guess, but it sounds more like a name, to me. It's not much stranger than Lloyd. Now there's a name I could never figure out, looking at it written." Laurie turns on the night-table lamp and crosses the room to turn off the overhead before getting into bed. She yawns.

"Same with Ian."

"Anyway, I'm glad he knew what to do." Dan steps out of his trousers, tucks the waistband under his chin, and slides them onto a hanger, then gropes for the rod in the dark closet. "I looked useless, in an emergency. I'm surprised at how long I took to even realize it *was* an emergency."

If the Sahasrabudis hadn't shown up, he thinks, he might have spent the rest of the summer dumping bales of hay or something into the pool, whatever moose eat. But Deepak had materialized in the yard, waving his arms above his head and laughing. Saruda floated behind him, weightless in a gold-edged, lilac sari, her mouth covered with both hands. When the five of them lined up poolside they presented the solemn appearance of jurors, a random selection of humanity gathered to common purpose. The moose looked judicious. Its small eyes fixed on each of them in turn, and it snorted in a deep, pensive manner. Everyone stepped back. Saruda put her head close to her husband's and whispered something Dan couldn't hear.

"You must call the city," Deepak said.

"The city?" Dan repeated, for a moment thinking the phrase was a mnenomic—THE-CITY, like SEX-LINE or C0C-AINE.

"Oh," he caught on, "a municipal department."

No one answered at the numbers under *Animal* in the phone book's blue pages, although Dan wasn't sure what help he'd get there, since the sub-listings were *Disease* and *Export.* The latter, he thought, was a little more than was necessary; he wouldn't mention the other to Laurie.

After trying a few more numbers, picked almost at random, he ended up leaving a message with a man he imagined was a security guard, alone in City Hall on a Saturday night, pulled out of reverie by the phone chirruping and echoing in labyrinth corridors of glass and granite, fluorescent fixtures slick but lightless above quarry tile floors, only square EXIT signs visible above doors at hall endings. The man's voice went distant as soon as he heard, "I have a moose in my swimming pool." He sounded preoccupied and remote as he took down the address and—*"Yes. Uh-huh, sure"*—promised Dan something would be done first thing in the morning.

"They'll send somebody, I guess," Dan told Laurie. "Tomorrow."

"Good, good," she nodded, moving around the kitchen, taking things down from shelves and out of drawers. "Listen, I invited the Sahasrabudis for dinner. I mean, they're already *here.* Why don't you see if they want drinks, then set up the deck while I get started? Josh can carry things out for you." She gasped and held up the meat mallet. "What could I have been *thinking?* They must be Muslim or Hindu or something. I can't give them *veal.*"

"Pizza," Dan said, picking up the phone again. He tapped out the number in seven firm punches. Laurie didn't look properly impressed with his decisiveness. He covered the receiver with one hand and added, with the brevity of someone disturbed during an international call, "Vegetarian special."

Dan pushes his underwear down to his ankles, steps out and kicks up, catching and tossing it towards the hamper in one fluid move, where it hits the swing-top and disappears from sight. He raises his arms over his head and says, "He scores."

"Uh-huh, how much excitement can you take in one day?" Laurie asks.

"Not a lot," he admits, pulling back the sheet on his side of the bed. When he drops onto the mattress, his lungs empty in a long sigh. He raises his upper body. "Do you hear anything?"

"No?"

"Remember last month?"

"June?" Laurie shakes her head. "I don't remember anything special happening last month."

"Yeah, that's what I mean." Dan slaps his pillow a few times to flatten it, and turns to face her. His shoulder peaks up under the sheet; the cotton drapes down into a valley between them. He bends one leg so his knee touches her hip. "I'm starting to think of it very, very fondly."

Later, he wakes with a gasp, as though he'd stopped breathing. In the dark room he listens to the sounds of the house settling, the continuous whir of the heat pump circulating cool air through the rooms. He's too lethargic to get up and look out the window—he has one arm bent under the pillow beneath his head, his legs crossed at the ankles—but no noise comes to him from the outside. He keeps his eyes open until he can feel himself sliding into sleep. His last conscious thought is of Saruda. As the light faded she seemed to become invisible, vanishing into the night until her presence was defined only by the dull gleam of her gold rings, the thin bracelets on her arms. She hardly spoke two words the whole evening. He has no memory of the sound of her voice.

"He slept like a horse," Joshua says. "He just stayed standing up all night. At least, I guess he was sleeping, he wasn't trying to get out or anything. And he stopped making that noise."

"He didn't snore?" Dan asks, looking over at Laurie. She's standing in front of the sink with her back to him. He raises his voice, over the sound of the water she's running into an enamelled saucepan. "He didn't kick his hooves around and take up all the room in the pool?"

"Huh?"

Joshua picks up a toast soldier and dips it into his soft-boiled egg. The narrow strip of bread folds into pleats as he stuffs it into his mouth. A thick drop of yolk smears over his chin. Dan cracks the top off his own egg, a little too low, and looks down at the bull's eye of yellow in white. He thinks, *pre-chicken,* then uses his spoon to scoop out the egg and spreads it over a piece of toast where it loses any suggestion it might have had of wholeness.

Laurie cuts off the water and says, "We have company."

"The neighbours?" Dan gets up and goes over to the window. Two men he's never seen before are crossing the backyard, toward the pool. One of the men has a camera with a long lens hanging from one shoulder and a square, black case hanging from the other. The second man appears unburdened. Both are wearing plaid shirts and grey cords. They look, he thinks, like outside scrutineers, the ones who make sure their candidate gets voted in and then seem to vanish from the political scene until the next election.

"I'd better see what they want." Dan is reluctant about confronting them; he's not anxious, merely wary. It's the same feeling he has when he answers the door and is facing a couple of religious types; a failure to communicate is inevitable. But even before he's halfway across the lawn, the man without the camera identifies himself and introduces his friend. They're from the newspaper. Whoever answered the phone at City Hall called them first, although the newsman assures Dan help is on the way. He doesn't say who the help is for, Dan or the moose, but it adds up to the same thing. The moose puts its head back and sniffs at the air. The cameraman clicks off three or four frames in quick succession. He doesn't move his thumb between pictures. Even though Dan didn't hear any electronic whine, he guesses the camera is motor-driven.

"They're from the paper," Dan calls. Laurie and Joshua have come out to the deck. "Come on down."

"Get the kid," the newsman tells the cameraman as Joshua approaches.

"Joshua," Dan says.

"Hey, Josh. Want to get your picture in the paper?"

"Is it okay?" he asks.

Dan nods. Laurie is already beside her son, smoothing his hair down and tucking his T-shirt into his shorts. She looks up at Dan and mouths, *You see?*

"Pull up your socks," she tells Josh. Then, to the cameraman, "Where do you want him?"

"Up there, I think. Why don't you stand beside it?" He points to the shallow end. Then, to Dan, "Don't you want to be in the picture, Dad?"

"He's not my father," Joshua says quickly.

"That's right," Dan steps back. "Anyway, you know what they say. It's only proper to have your name in the paper when you're born, get married, and when you die."

He glances over at the moose, but it's turned away from him.

"I guess you hear that a lot."

"Nope." The cameraman squats down and opens the black bag for a new lens. "Never heard that one before."

If Joshua hadn't attached himself to the newsmen—Neal had the camera, the other was Wayne—Dan might have. There was a police-band radio and a cellular phone in the car. Wayne made a call, letting Josh punch in the numbers. Dan stood beside the garage, fiddling with the end of the flatbed as though he were checking the lights. He'd already decided, without noticeably thinking about it, to call a pool company, once the moose was removed, and get them to come and do whatever needs to be done. He won't even finish the draining.

Within half an hour, a police car pulled up. The female officer seemed to know Wayne. She got out of the car and talked to him for a minute. From where he stood, Dan only heard, "Are you *serious?*" before the woman and her partner walked past him. On the way back to the car, passing him again, she said, "Guess I don't call this in as domestic violence."

Dan raised his empty hands, and his eyebrows, in a mute offer of assistance but, as it turned out, he wasn't really required. The police radioed for help and an hour later a large truck arrived. It was a tall, square vehicle, like the kind milkmen used to drive. By then the neighbours had started coming from their houses, to see what was causing all the traffic.

Now there's a crowd in the yard. Dan doesn't know half of the people standing around, but he's pleased to see that there are a few kids Joshua's age. They're in a clump at the shallow end of the pool, talking in loud voices and occasionally looking around at the grown-ups, like they wish they would evaporate. Dan remembers the feeling. He moves to one side and waves at the Sahasrabudis. They're in their own yard.

In the pool, two men walk up to the moose and, with no hesitation, pass a strap under its belly, part of a harness that looks like a seatbelt, only wider, and cinch the works. There's a kind of stirrup—a thick, silver-coloured ring—at the top of the harness that makes Dan think of steamer trunks. The moose grunts, but doesn't move.

A different noise makes everyone look up. The sound, a rhythmic *rhup rhup,* is familiar from the opening of a thousand episodes of M*A*S*H. A helicopter comes into view over the rim of trees at the far edge of the Parkway.

Everyone in the yard goes, "Aaah." As the helicopter hovers overhead, churning up air, a few shield their eyes with their hands. Dan senses their movement and turns to see Saruda lift the edge of her sari to cover her face. In that moment, everything else about the situation seems to him entirely normal: the non-functioning swimming pool, the trapped moose, a yard full of strangers *and* Joshua, all of it seems, expressly, Canadian. Only the dark-skinned woman, clad in an outfit unavailable at the Bay, or Eaton's, or Holt-Renfrew, protecting herself from the grit raised by a helicopter's rotor; only that image is foreign to him, an image as remote as war. Were he standing closer to Josh, he knows he would say, "Everything'll be all right." He'd have to add, "But I can't say that for sure. I can't promise anything."

When the hook at the end of the rope lowered from the helicopter is snapped into the ring of the harness, one of the men standing in the pool quickly slips a burlap bag over the moose's head, then tugs the rope, two jerks, signalling the pilot to gain altitude.

"Cover their eyes that way and it's like they're sedated," he explains to Dan, after the moose has been carried off. "Same with crocs."

"That's interesting," Dan says, refusing to consider a crocodile loose anywhere in the city, but especially not in his own backyard. "I'm really sorry you had to come out like this, on a Sunday. I have to apologize for the inconvenience."

"Are you crazy, inconvenience?" The man laughs. "Christ, we're on double-time. You get another moose coming through that fence, you wait until the weekend to pitch him into the pool. Get it?"

"Got it." And when he repeats it to Laurie, Dan says, "It had crossed my mind. Was I supposed to be out there handing out five-dollar bills?" She looked confused and he amended, "Twenties?"

Dan wasn't home the two afternoons it took for the pool to be repaired, so he doesn't know how much effort it required. He made out the cheque to Neptune of Ottawa with some satisfaction. He could afford it, and he couldn't help noting the total wasn't much more than he and Laurie would spend on a weekend in Toronto, seeing a play and doing some shopping. That done, he called Sears and arranged for the shattered wooden fence to be replaced with chainlink, six feet high. Another cheque. The small voice in his head, the voice that sounds like his father's, mumbled only *that's a lot of bucks,* but not *too* much. Next year, he might have the yard re-sodded. It probably won't recover from being flooded and trampled.

"This is good," he tells Laurie. "Having a place for Josh to bring his friends." If nothing else, in their company Joshua looks...like a *member.*

"I was a little worried, at first." Laurie lowers her voice. "About Brent."

"The blond lad?"

"Don't point. You must have noticed he has that crusty skin around his nose. I was afraid it was drugs, but I was talking to his mother and it's only allergies."

"Doesn't hurt to be careful," Dan says. He won't tell her

about his own suspicion that Joshua was taking beer from the fridge when he went out in the evenings. He waited until he started a new twelve-pack and kept track of the bottles, full and empty. They were all accounted for. He was almost ashamed of himself.

A light breeze, cooling even in August, carries the kids' voices away from him. He can't make out what they're saying. They don't sound excited or high-spirited, but it's enough that they're talking, however laconic and deliberately cool. They never go swimming, but stretch out around the water like walrus at the edge of the sea. For all that Josh talks about the hole in the ozone layer, Dan has never seen him use sunscreen. The girls, Lisa and Eve, may put it on at home, under their makeup.

From the deck, he can see the smoothness of their bodies, each one separate, each healthy and young. This afternoon is theirs to define, and it's enough for Dan if nothing more happens, nothing memorable. Days can slip, seamlessly, one into another, from now until school starts. A moment later he realizes that Josh won't be here in September. He glances at his watch. The boy leaves in less than two weeks. Dan tries to figure out his response, emotionally, but he's thinking rather than feeling. He tries *relief,* then *loss.* Either seems overstated, the space between them too wide for examination.

Inside the airport, later that month, Laurie will take Joshua up to the check-in counter while Dan stands a little to one side, waiting until they're at the head of the line so he can put Josh's suitcase on the scale. Once he has it lifted up onto the dull metal plate, he'll walk around a bit and find a place to sit on a low, vinyl-covered bench, with his back to a huge expanse of window.

Everyone who walks by looks anxious and harried, not at all like vacationers. One man has a newspaper folded under his arm. Dan reads part of a bold headline: *Airbus Disaster.* He looks away and sees Laurie point him out to the woman at the counter. He raises his hand with his index finger pointing up. The woman picks up a phone and speaks into it. Joshua heads off down the corridor. Laurie comes over to him.

"He's gone to the washroom," she says. "They've called the flight crew. Someone is supposed to come down here to take him to the boarding area."

"We don't do that?"

"Apparently not."

"I kind of thought we'd take him right to his seat." Dan waves away the image in his mind, of the two of them standing in the aisle, looking on as a stewardess shows Josh how to pull his lap belt tight before she straightens up and faces them with a wide, reassuring smile. There are no other passengers on the plane and the interior is as generously vast as a cathedral. "This just seems awfully casual."

"Well, this is how things are done."

"You're certainly *handling* this well," Dan says, unable to hide the edge in his tone. "Don't you feel anything?"

"Don't you tell me how to feel about this." Laurie squints into the harsh light coming over Dan's shoulder.

"He's just breezing in and out of your life, this summer, but he's *my son.* It's a women's thing. I don't expect you to understand."

Without turning his head, Dan tries to sense if people are staring, but he registers no feeling of being on display, probably he looks no different than any other traveller. He has nothing to say. Not now.

"Listen, can you wait here by yourself? I think I should get him something to read on the plane. Maybe a deck of cards or something. There's a little shop around the corner. Here, take the boarding pass, in case they ask for it."

Dan watches her walk away. At the point where the corridor widens into a hub ringed by a snack bar, news stand, rental car agencies, he sees her turn to the right and stop, standing still. A moment later she's joined by Joshua. The two of them don't turn back, but move off to the left. Laurie has her hands in front of her, higher than her waist, describing something in the air. Dan sees Josh laugh before they disappear behind an arc of ceramic tile. He follows, with his eyes, a line in the floor's pattern, from there to where his feet are.

"Are you the unaccompanied minor?"

The man who's spoken is standing in front of Dan. He's younger, about thirty, wearing dark blue trousers and a white nylon shirt, snug-fitting and nearly transparent. A plastic bar tagged to the pocket says *Marc.* He's carrying a clipboard. He repeats, "Unaccompanied minor?" on a sliding note and smiles. His teeth are so white they're almost silver.

"Yes, that's me," Dan says, feeling he should stand, but

not having enough room unless he first slides to one side. Otherwise, they'd bump noses.

"Has anyone told you, you look very old for your age?"

"Well, not *me,* but...."

"A little joke, there, but if you could give me a bit of information about who I'm going to be looking after?"

Instead of sitting beside Dan, Marc hunkers down in front of him, like a shoe salesman, with the clipboard over his knees. Dan is looking down the line of his back. Above the trousers, through the shirt, he can see a band of white elastic. In the middle of this is a green label the size of a postage stamp. His eyes keep returning to it as he answers questions about Joshua's flight, his connections and his vegetarian meal. No medical problems. No allergies.

"And on arrival?" Marc glances up. "Who's meeting your son?"

"He's not my son," Dan shakes his head. "His father will be meeting him."

"He's not? Well, I guess I have everything I need to know." Marc stands up, holding the clipboard against his chest. "Now, can I take him up to boarding?"

"His mother took him to get a magazine. They should be right back." As he says this, he rises to his feet. He's a little taller than Marc, so he slouches a bit and leans forward, keeping his voice down. "This is absolutely none of my business," he says. "But I think you have your underpants on inside-out."

"These kind have the label on the outside," Marc says, without hesitation. "I have some others where it's here." He touches, with his plastic pen, a point about an inch below his belt buckle, then laughs. "I can't do much with this uniform, so I'm individualistic underneath. Being a flight attendant isn't all about glamour."

"But it must be exciting. All that flying. New places."

"Listen, I spend my layovers in hotels. It's a rough world out there. My apartment is here, downtown. And, believe me, flying isn't everything. It's no home sweet home in the sky. I have much more fun on the ground."

"Me, too, I guess," Dan says, not at all sure what he means. "At least, I'm not going anywhere."

But today, before that happens, Joshua walks over to the deck and says, "Can I have some money for the mall?"

Dan says, "Sure," at the same time Laurie asks, "How much?"

"I don't know. Thirty-five dollars?"

"What? That's an awful lot of money. What do you want it for?"

"Well, you know, stuff. I mean, there's cab fare, both ways. And we might do a movie. Then I want a gelato and a beaver tail."

"Don't overdo it," Dan says. "I'm making zucchini boats for dinner."

"I don't think it would kill you to take the bus," Laurie says. "Do you know how long I have to work to make thirty-five dollars?"

"About an hour." Josh shrugs. "Hey, I don't think it'll break you."

"That's not the issue here." Laurie's voice has gone flat; she's being reasonable. "I don't think your father hands out sums like that, and I don't think he'd want me to, either. You're old enough to learn the value of money. You might even think about getting a job of your own, next summer."

"That's *then.*" Josh starts to whine. "Geez, I can't even go to the mall without you making some big production out of it."

Dan has tuned out. His head is back; he's staring up at the sky. He's trying to feel his stomach pressed against a webbed nylon strap, his legs dangling in space. In the air, the moose's legs had hung straight down, as rigid as prosthetic devices. He doesn't know what he'd expected, seeing a moose's hooves from underneath, but he suspects it might have been horseshoes. What he knows has limits. He'll never think of everything.

He closes his eyes. The sun is warm on his face. Would the moose have known it was being saved? Was there terror in the moment it was pulled away from the hard, wet floor of the pool? Or did it—does any creature—feel exhilaration in that single moment unlike any other? The animal's placid demeanour may have hidden a panic of confusion; it may have been paralysed by possibility. Or it may have been quieted by a profound concentration, memorizing.

Laurie and Joshua will eventually come to a conclusion, possibly an agreement. Someone may be angry, someone's feelings hurt, whatever. This matters, but only a little. Dan doesn't have to pay attention. He's not with them, not on the ground. Even with a burlap bag over his head, he thinks, he'd thrill to the dislocation. He wouldn't know where he was going, but he'd thrill to the freedom of being carried away.

. . . because

When Phil was in grade ten, his parents split up and his mother moved the family to an apartment in the suburbs. His sister, Alison, had graduated that spring, and was taking a special one-year secretarial course at the High School of Commerce, closer to downtown. Phil hadn't made any real friends, yet, although he knew *of* people, those who were *known* in high school. He knew who the Head Boy and Girl were, who was on the football team and who were cheerleaders. He knew that Karen Feores was adopted. Randy Scarlett was a dealer, and kept marijuana in his locker's hollow coatpole. Kevin Reid's brother had died of leukaemia. Janice Martin had run away during the summer, getting as far as Montreal before her parents tracked her down and lured her home with the promise of a '68 Maverick. She got a hardtop in Hula Blue, which most of the school considered a disappointing, conservative choice. Phil thinks there was a Mellow Yellow, or Electric Banana, but he can't remember the hype name for the consensus—red.

He rode OTC in the morning, living a block short of the cut-off for the school bus. Most days, he walked home.

At lunch time, the third week in September, he took a seat at an almost-full table of kids he recognized, but couldn't name; some girls from the four-year program, a couple of guys who took bookkeeping. He nodded at the faces around him, noticing a girl from his last period art class was sitting at the far end, apparently by herself. He put his brown bag down and, with a thumb and finger on each of the bottom corners, pulled the bag away like a magician stripping away a table cloth, leaving the setting intact.

It wasn't much of a trick, and Phil became slightly nervous as silence fell over the table, a silence that spread through the cafeteria. He looked around the room. He looked down at the table.

In front of him were two very red and shiny apples. And, between them, the largest and whitest sanitary napkin in the history of feminine protection. No way was there any ambiguity, no possibility that he had been carrying something from a first-aid kit in case of a scholarly accident, a paper cut, or a puncture from the sharp point of a compass. There was enough fluffed wood pulp in front of him to make a mattress for G.I. Joe on shore leave.

Phil slipped into a kind of low grade shock. It wouldn't bother him, now, to call across three aisles in the drugstore, "The ribbed ones don't have nonoxynol, should I get half a dozen anyway?" At least, it wouldn't bother him until he got home, then he'd feel the way he does when he finds out he's been walking around with his fly open.

But not much before he was in grade ten, he'd been baffled by the advertisements in the back pages of his mother's magazines. A dark-haired woman, jewelled and gowned, stood at the top of a broad, stone staircase outside a palatial residence lit with the soft tones of expensive privacy. A white limousine was poised at the end of the circular drive. In the bottom right-hand corner of the photograph, discreetly lower case:

modess

. . . because

The gown, the jewels and the car were all too softly focussed for something being promoted. The woman's face was too indistinct to be advertising cosmetics. Phil concluded that the picture represented a service rather than a product, but it seemed unlikely that a limousine company would advertise in the back pages of *Good Housekeeping* and *Redbook.* If they did, they'd include a phone number, and there wasn't one.

He had decided, finally, that *modess* was a dry cleaning technique, like Martinizing.

All his life he's been surrounded by cryptic images. As a photographer, he's created some enigmatic images of his own. But that one remains discrete in his mind, an unanswered question:

. . . because

Because *what?*

He pushed the pad and apples back in the bag. He tossed the works into the garbage on his way out of the cafeteria, left the building and crossed the teachers' parking lot to the smoking area where he bummed an Export A from Pete Mallory, the hairiest guy in grade nine, two years running.

With the day almost over, Phil climbed the stairs to the art room, a large, loft-like space above the school's centre foyer. It's location removed it from the other classrooms. In other ways, it created its own reality.

The art teacher's name was Wendy Clarke. The year before she'd been a college student and this was her first assignment. She was a little unconventional for the suburbs. She didn't live in the neighbourhood, and she didn't look like anyone who did.

Instead of long-sleeved, belted wool dresses like Mrs. Perry, or straight skirts with jackets open over white blouses like Miss Antonelli, Miss Clarke wore thin Indian cotton tops from Orientique, a suede miniskirt, dark tights and ballet slippers.

She wore glasses with eight-sided, rimless lenses, and played records that she brought from home, not classical stuff borrowed from the music teacher.

She looked cool.

"*Learn* your other subjects," she'd said the first day. "In this room, I want you to *do* art."

She said far-out things.

She looked like no one Phil had ever seen until he saw a movie with subtitles. Her hair, cut nearly as short as Phil's was long, changed colour almost weekly. At the crown, where the part ended, there was a patch, about the size of a silver dollar, that was always the next-to-last colour.

She was *unreal.*

When he's older, in his twenties, Phil decides that everything means something else; it's all connected. His own age was a recapitulation of the new Age of Man. He'd stop eating meat, and bake his own bread. He and the world were moving towards some higher consciousness. He used to say things like that. What people are saying now is: Shit happens.

At the time, he only wanted Miss Clarke to like him—he wanted to *be* someone she would like—and he spent his time doing the two things he did admirably: pen-and-ink drawings of constellations of mushrooms, or watercolours of goldfish. He thought it might be time for a new challenge, however, and was contemplating the artistic merit of tracing his own hands when the girl who'd been at the lunchtable slid into the desk beside his.

"Here," she said, passing him half a Kit-Kat, two joined chocolate fingers. "I thought you might be hungry."

That was Margaret. Phil always had some sense of that moment, or an expectation of a moment like that one, when he'd meet her again over the next two decades: when he'd end up back in Ottawa (after his parents tried a reconciliation that didn't take); working at summer jobs during university; returning from a couple of months in Paris, where he'd gone to see the light. Perfect for painters, he decided, but he couldn't do a thing with it. And the people there were a good argument for the neutron bomb.

He and Margaret never had to make any special effort to keep in touch, not sending change-of-address cards or checking the listings when the new telephone books were delivered in February. Sooner or later, they'd run into each other.

One time he got off the number 7 bus at Bank and Laurier, almost knocking her down as she rushed past to catch a 4. She called out her new address and invited him to come over on the weekend, naming a time that might or might not have meant he was being invited for dinner.

He arrived at the Sandy Hill walk-up fifteen minutes early, carrying a cone of carnations dyed palest blue, to discover she and the man she was living with were hosting a Grey Cup party.

He sat on the couch, drinking beer, and pretended to focus on the television. On the small screen, overpaid drug addicts risked their bones and joints, all they had to offer the world. Well, he supposed, what *else* could they do?

His glance kept moving around the room, furtive and assessing. He was searching for the commonalities between this experience and any events available in his memory. Finding a match would let him know how to respond.

At half-time he had nothing to say to anyone and started gathering up paper plates and napkins. He carried everything into the kitchen and asked Margaret what else needed to be done.

She directed him to a room at the bottom of the stairs. Phil stopped at the last landing, vibrant with prickles of recognition. There had been a very similar one in the basement of the building where his mother had moved him and his sister. On the left, at the bottom of the stairs, was the room with the coin-operated washing machines and dryers. Across from it was a locked room where the janitor kept his supplies. The hall went straight for a couple of yards, with tenants' lockers on either side. It was crossed by a shorter hall of lockers, like the bar of a T, then continued down to the garbage room. The walls were painted a pale pink, rather than mint green, but it was somehow the same *colour.* Landlord Pastel.

And Phil remembered, in his mother's place, rolling on the floor in front of the television, whining about having nothing to do.

"I'm so *bored.*" He stretched the word out into a deep lowing, cow-like and plaintive. *"Booored."*

"I don't understand why you're both home on a Friday night," Mrs. Peddles said, looking up from her decorating magazine, her palm marking a pictorial article headed *Harvest the New Golds.* Interior design was her new passion. The apartment was in a permanent state of flux. She kept trying new arrangements of furniture and replacing end-tables and lamps and things called "throw pillows" so that, some days, Phil came home to a room entirely different from the one he left in the morning. Even the kitchen cutlery couldn't be taken for granted, which drawer it would be in.

"Surely there's something going on," she said. "A movie?"

"I'm going out later," Alison said. She'd changed after dinner and was wearing a blue mini-dress with a wide chain belt. She had her hair tied up in rags, white bows of torn-up bedsheet. A year earlier she'd been setting it with orange-juice tins, making her face look shrunken and helpless, like some tiny mammal whose only defence against predators is a sudden ballooning. One of Phil's summer jobs during college was at an office with a woman who'd worked with Alison a year earlier, at Computrack. "I always thought of your sister," she confided, "as the kind of woman whose hair dryer would have *attachments.*" Phil agreed enthusiastically, although he wasn't sure what she meant.

"Nothing happens until after nine," Alison stated.

"Nine? Like the late show, you mean?"

"She means, when the Hell's Angels finish their jobs at *garages,*" Phil snickered, then rolled over onto his stomach. *"Booored."*

"Well, don't be too late. I'm not waiting up past one."

"Maybe, if I had my own key," Alison said, "you wouldn't have to."

"This isn't a hotel. It's your home and we don't sail in and out like strangers at all hours."

"Boooooooooored."

"Can't you do something with your brother before you go out?" Mrs. Peddles asked. "You used to like Monopoly." A hesitancy, or diffidence, in her tone arced across the room, silencing her children. She didn't have anything to do, either. She may have had even fewer options.

With the unexamined complicity of siblings, that rare, unpredictable sensitivity, he was on his feet as soon as his sister said, "Come on, the board is in the locker. I'll let you be banker if I get the roller skate."

At the bottom of the stairs, purely by chance, Phil noticed that the door to the janitor's closet wasn't entirely closed.

"Hey," he said softly, but Alison didn't hear and kept walking. Phil pushed the door open and stepped into the small space. He didn't tug on the ball-link chain hanging from the ceiling. There was enough light from the hall behind him to illuminate the room. Everything looked beaten-up and dirty: the mop and bucket, the concrete cast sink, even the shelf of industrial-sized cleaning products, household names made unfamiliar by the containers' mass. And—Phil's hand reached out even before he was aware of registering the detail—a package of mousetraps.

He tore open the cellophane wrapping and set the first trap, using his thumb to hold down the U-shaped jaw attached to a spring, tucking the fine lever under the trap plate as though he'd been doing this every day of his life.

He stepped back into the hall, to show Alison what he'd found. She had the locker open, in the centre of the cross hall directly in front of him, and was bent over the raised lid of a blue metal trunk. Phil warned her with a quiet, "I can't help it," as he tossed the trap at her, underhand and without much force. He heard the solid *thwick* of the sprung trap and his sister's gratifying squeal and, in the same moment, he set a second trap.

"What are you—stop it!"

"I can't, I can't," Phil said, swinging his arm back and forth slowly, warming up his shoulder. "Run, run. Quick like a bunny."

Unspoken, rules were established. They knew what to do.

Alison would run along the hall, left to right, right to left, and while she was visible, he'd toss the set traps at her. Five, he'd toss; he held the sixth in reserve, set, for self-defence when he charged forward to reclaim the sprung traps, none of which attached themselves to Alison's dress or stockings. They merely snapped against her body, *thwick,* and dropped to the floor.

After a few trials, they were both wound-up and shrieking, nearly hysterical and unable to stop.

"Let's give up," Alison would shout, from the safety of the side hall. "That's enough, okay?"

"Okay. Yeah," Phil would agree. But then, when she came into range, he was powerless to resist the impulse, his *need* to pitch one more trap.

Thwick.

"Phillip!"

"I'm *sorry,*" Phil said, helplessly, indefensibly. "Save yourself."

It took nearly an hour, and the disappearance of one of the traps through the narrow slats of a locker door, before they were able to call it quits for real, leaning against opposite wall in the hall, breathless and shiny with sweat.

Now Phil wonders, *What the hell was* that *about?* but he can't imagine who he'd ask for an explanation, who he'd tell, even. Maybe someone paid to listen, although probably not a bartender. Certainly not before last call.

By Christmas, Phil couldn't entirely recall how the school had seemed so strange to him. He went from one class to the next, feeling his passage through the halls was inevitable, unable to recapture his former sense of confusion, his panic that he would get lost. At lunchtime he joined the group in the outside smoking area, huddled around the old oil drum, used as a garbage can, like it was a source of heat.

After school he was part of a gang that trekked along Merivale Road—a line of bodies leaning into the wind against the snowy background like prisoners being marched to Siberia—going to the K-Mart for ginger ale and french fries with gravy. They had to leave their books at the front of the store and someone walked off with Phil's history text a week before the Easter exam. He didn't bother to replace it. His mother had announced that they would be moving in July and he thought, if he failed the class, he'd leave the lousy grade behind and start over. Sometime during the year he'd stopped being convinced of the idea of a permanent record. It wasn't relevant.

Miss Clarke had outdone herself in setting up the art room for her exam. Sheets of aluminum foil were twisted into loose spirals and taped to the room's upper corners. The silver rolled gently as waves over two walls. A third wall, opposite the door, served as a screen for projected slides of street signs: *One Way. Do Not Enter. Stop.*

In the language of the day, this was a *happening.*

At the end of the room there was a ladder. Taped to one of its uprights was a small drawing of an eagle in flight, captioned "Bird's eye view."

Phil promptly climbed as high as he could, his head

almost bumping the ceiling. Everyone else was sitting down. Miss Clarke was circling the room, coming closer. He didn't know what to do next. He couldn't come down until he, somehow, validated climbing up in the first place. His action had to be turned into Art.

With Miss Clarke standing beside the ladder, her head a little lower than the level of his knees, he was on the verge of confessing his failure to transform the experience. The record that had been playing ended and a new album dropped onto the turntable. The low, dirty, opening of "Hurdy Gurdy Man" rolled through the room.

"I *love* this song," he said, looking down at his teacher, glad of the distraction. The last-dyed section of her hair was an ashen spot in a golden surround.

"Me, too," she said. "It's really sexy."

Phil, dizzied, clutched the ladder. When Miss Clarke moved on, he had to make an effort to loosen his grip. The tips of his fingers were white. He flexed his hands on his way to the supply cabinet for a sheet of best-quality paper, like a pianist warming up. He knew what he was going to do.

The picture would be divided into layers of colour, like a cut-away view of the world and the sky. At the bottom, there would be a field of inked mushrooms. Above them, at the top of the page, there would be a school of goldfish. Then bands of colour-wash; blue dark as the deep sea over the mushrooms, below bands of light brown, for the earth, then grass-green, and finally, around the fish, a pale sky-blue with the merest slice of bright sunshine.

This, he knew, would be his first mature work. He

would title it—he thrilled to the profundity and power of this name—*Surrealistic Garden.*

When the marks came out, he wasn't all that surprised to be head of the class.

"Do you know what Miss Clarke said, about why you got the highest mark?"

"No," he said, cautiously. "What did she say?"

"She said you were the only one who climbed up the ladder."

Phil was silenced, unable to sort out a response; he didn't know what his reaction *was.* He thought of Miss Clarke saying "sexy." He thought of her talking to Margaret. About him. He had too much information and not enough knowledge.

He had had the same feeling when he ran into Margaret years later at the Royal Bank on Sparks Street. He'd moved back from Kingston and was transferring his account, as well as a student loan that had taken on the magnitude of a mortgage. She was married to Stan by then, and had a little boy named Steven. They were too loud for the bank and headed down the Mall to Sharry's.

Margaret told him that the morning after Steven was born, Stan showed up at the hospital with a pair of leather jeans he'd bought himself. "The clerk said I could just cut them to length," he'd said, spreading the slacks over the end of her bed, avoiding her feet, "but I stopped at that hobby shop on O'Connor and got an awl and some gut so you could give them a proper hem."

Phil listened to the story, waiting to hear the word *divorce,* but Margaret didn't mention it for another five years. During that time, when he'd meet Stan, Phil would think, *Be nice. I* know *things.*

But knowing isn't the same as understanding. Possibly the real point was merely that Stan got what he wanted: leather jeans. Maybe the story was about desire.

When Phil was fifteen, what he had wanted was a skinny, ribbed sweater to wear over a pair of elephant pants with a six-button Navy front. His mother had dismissed the outfit as a fad.

"You'll want to see what the kids are wearing at your new school," she said. "I can't afford to buy you a whole wardrobe for one summer."

"Where are we moving, anyway," Phil protested, "the *moon?* Everyone will be wearing the same stuff. At least, the cool people will be."

"If everyone jumped off a bridge," Mrs. Peddles said complacently, "would you?"

Phil was enraged by her logic, or lack of it.

"The only guys jumping off *bridges* are the ones dressed like *dorks.*"

A song in constant play on the radio that summer suggested, if you were going to San Francisco, wear flowers in your hair. Phil wasn't going that far, but the spirit of the lyric was very much with him as he dressed.

At the Salvation Army store he'd found a regulation-sized Union Jack. He'd folded this in half, parallel to the staff-end, and sewn it together along three-quarters of the top edge. The open seam went over his head, and he bloused the fabric, poncho-like, over one of his sister's chain belts. The belt went under the flag at the back, so the silk flowed behind him like a cape. Like a... flag.

He wore this over a pair of jeans that he'd soaked in bleach in the laundry room tub downstairs. Something about the process was imperfect. The jeans were supposed to have come out soft and faded, as though from long wear. Instead, they were a scummy, or hazy, grey, almost not a colour at all. They looked like the bathwater after Alison had shaved her legs. Even this, however, was better than the too-blue of new Lee jeans.

"You're not going out like *that?*" his mother asked.

"Don't blow a gasket," Phil said, flapping through the yards of fabric to get his wallet into his back pocket. He looked at his reflection in the dresser mirror and decided to remove his headband (until moments before, the thin belt around the crown of his Scout hat). There was *too much,* which was good; and "too much," which wasn't. He rubbed at the small red mark where the buckle had pressed into his forehead. "I thought you'd be thrilled that this isn't what *everyone* will be wearing."

"Oh, wow." Alison stuck her head in the door.

"Get out of my room," Phil said. "You're not allowed in here."

He pushed past his sister and made his escape into the Friday night. Passing cars slowed down while he was waiting at the bus stop. Faces peered in his direction, faces blobby and moon-like behind the sky's reflection on windshields. Later, when he has an inkling that he might have looked ridiculous, he'll slant his memory instead, to the cool, liquid ripple of silk against his upper body on that breezy evening in late June.

What he can't remember is how he knew that Miss Clarke was having a party: he hadn't been invited. The details of time and place, somehow overheard, had come through the air and struck his grey cells like light striking silver nitrate, causing an instant reaction. A permanent record.

All summer Tina Turner has been offering to sell herself for Deutsche marks or dollars. Phil's listening to the song in the record store and, the way she sings it, the phrase still sounds to him like, "touch myself down there."

He waits, listening intently, then shakes his head and goes back to flipping through the delete bins for cheap cassettes, moving aside to let a mother and son team reach a rack of special-compilation discs. The woman is wearing a leather bomber jacket and sweat pants. No makeup. A closer look reveals the jacket to be vinyl. He thinks she looks about forty, then concedes that probably means she's about his own age, some five years younger. Her son is dressed in similar style, with the addition of a dangling earring that looks like fish parts, scales and bones. He may be fourteen or fifteen. Phil doesn't know kids' ages; none of what he sees seems equivalent to anything he's been through.

"Mom, look at this," the boy says, holding up one of the over-sized boxes discs are packed in, long and wide enough to hold a necktie from the Sixties. "Did you know that George Harrison used to be in a *group.*"

"You've broken my heart, Dylan," the woman says. "If I wasn't in labour for twenty-six hours, I'd swear you were adopted."

At the reference to time, Phil glances at his watch. He leaves the few cassettes he'd chosen—classics like Grassroots and Percy Sledge—and heads out into the street. Three ninety-nine sounds cheap only until you pay it four or five times. His sister may be right when she says he doesn't know the value of a dollar, but he has a healthy respect for a twenty.

Peripherally, he sees his jacket and jeans walking towards him, somehow distorted and suspended, like a fly in amber. He stops and turns. The video store has a camcorder aimed at the sidewalk. He's looking at himself on a large-screen monitor. When he looks into the camera he can see himself face-on. If he looks at the screen, he's in three-quarter profile.

The effect is disconcerting and he thinks, This has nothing to do with real life. But he notes that the cameras are getting smaller and more affordable. He can imagine a future in which no one has any personal memories, only shelves loaded with cassettes containing their pasts, records as sterile and unevocative as a legal transcript.

He looks past the display, into the store. A man and a woman are standing in front of a glass counter, aiming cameras at each other. Each has the eye that's not at the viewfinder scrunched shut.

The future is now. And here he is.

Behind him, still dancing for money, Tina offers to do the shimmy again. She sounds threatening and compliant, both at once. Phil can't imagine how he'd react to her in person. Some things never change.

After leaving the record store, Phil went to an underground mall off Queen Street, where Margaret has a shop. She sells lingerie, scraps of silk and satin (or Qiana and acetate) with skinny straps and laces—stuff you'd have to see on a woman to know what it *was*. The shop is called *Mlle. B.* and a poster of Sarah Bernhardt costumed as Phaedre is the only display in the window. Phil can't imagine what first-time customers are expecting, what draws them in.

He waited until he was sure no one was browsing inside before he slipped through the door, managing not to glance back over his shoulder. Margaret was behind the small desk that held the cash register, telephone, and a credit-card machine. She was wearing thick cotton gloves and using a mean-looking tool, like a lino knife, to cut through the taped edges of corrugated cardboard boxes.

Phil watched her for a while before he said, "I think you want to invest in a new blade, that one looks pretty dull."

"I have a whole box of them, but I don't want to use one that's sharp enough to cut through my gloves." Margaret looked up at him a moment later and said, "Don't listen to me, I'm not making much sense these days."

"Here," Phil said, holding out his hand. "Can I?"

Now they're carrying the cut-down boxes to the garbage. This should not be surprising, Phil thinks, but it's a discovery to him that the underground shops are backed by a shadow-world of corridors for service access. Carrying the sheets of cardboard the way he'd carry a window, he follows Margaret down a hall with cinder-block walls painted a pale colour, a leisure-suit green.

"I don't know what this means about my character, but I'm really finding it difficult, having to tell people," she says, rattling the keys to the sliding gate she'd locked over the storefront when they left. "I'd expected, when I was pregnant, to be a little embarrassed about it in public, having everybody know something so personal about me. But I didn't have to *tell* anyone, not once I was showing. Then, of course, people would always ask me when I was due, which was sort of the other end, away from the private part, so that was all right."

"Uh-huh." Phil flips the cardboard up and over the edge of a large dumpster. He dusts his hands against his thighs. "Sorry, but I'm not really sure what you're telling me here. You're expecting?"

"No, no. Thank god, no. Didn't I say? I'm leaving Stan."

Phil registers that—"leaving" rather than "left"—and murmurs an all-purpose, "That's too bad." His tact inflates him. He's light-headed with his own sensitivity.

"This is for the best," Margaret says. "I should have done it years ago, the very first time I found out what he was doing with my pantyhose."

"I don't think you want to tell me this," Phil interrupts.

"You don't have to defend him." Margaret's eyes narrow. "He never liked you."

"He never liked me?" Phil is unaccountably crushed. His mind automatically aborts *pantyhose* and turns to the real issue. Stan doesn't even know him. He's not entitled to an opinion. Why would he express one? And how?

The day begins like any other. Margaret gets up and quietly checks on Stevie, who's kicked off his blankets and is sitting up in a corner of his crib, cuddling a large stuffed bear. He's dry. Margaret goes to the kitchen and plugs in the percolator, having prepared it with water and coffee the night before. While the coffee brews, she sets up a tray with mugs and croissants, then carries it into the bedroom and places it on the dresser, nudging aside a five-by-seven photograph in a silver-plated frame. She pulls back the curtains. Sunshine streams into the room, already rich with coffee fragrance. Stan awakes, rolling over onto his back. He covers his open eyes with one arm, slowing his entry into the new day.

"Good morning, my darling dumpling," Margaret says. "It's a gorgeous day out there. Let's do something special. We could pack a nice lunch and drive up to Kingsmere, or go to that pine place in Almonte. What do you think?"

"Both sound good. You decide, lambchop," Stan says. He yawns and rubs his jaw. "I don't like Phil. Never have."

"Okay," Phil tells Margaret. "Trash the mother." His laugh following this imperative leaves no room for her response. He laughs again, to hear the noise reverberate in the walled corridor. What he's listening to is the sound of a moment dropping into place.

If Miss Clarke was surprised to see him, she recovered smoothly, waving him into her apartment with a warming enthusiasm.

"I'm glad somebody's here," she said, backing down the short hall toward the kitchen. "I guess everyone else decided to be fashionably late."

"I'm pretty punctual," Phil said. He tried to correct for the too-fussy, schoolish sound of 'punctual' by adding, "It was the bus, really, that was on time. All I had to do with it was being there when it came."

She turned to look at him, the wall sconces of the kitchen nook reflecting off her glasses so he couldn't read her expression. Hearing himself, he thought he sounded demented. He shut up.

Despite her statement, that Phil was the first to arrive, there was a man in the kitchen. He was wearing a white shirt with the sleeves rolled up to his elbows, and was using a small knife with a serrated blade to cut up some lemons. He was wearing a tie, grey slacks with a leather belt and—Phil peeked down—black shoes. With a swirly design of perforations. Narc shoes. Waving the knife at Phil, the man said, "We'll have to skip the shake thing. My hands are all sticky. Hi."

"Hello," Phil said, the flag rippling over his upper body as he returned the wave. The man looked expectant, but Phil couldn't think of anything to add.

"It's hi," the man repeated.

Phil merely nodded, not wanting to get into an endless loop, like responding to the letter his grandmother sends him acknowledging receipt of his thank-you note for his birthday present. The three of them were very close in the tiny room, almost touching. The two men had to stand back a bit from the counter, to keep from bumping their heads on the cabinets. Phil could hear his own breathing and he looked over at Miss Clarke, helpless to break the impasse.

"My manners," she said, twisting a corkscrew into a bottle of red wine. "Hy, this is Phil. He was my top student this year. Phil, this is my, uh, Hy. And," she passed him a glass of wine, about a quarter full, "I'm Wendy."

"Oh, *Hy,*" Phil said. *"Hy.* Hi." He took a sip of the wine and felt his gums contract, but he thought he managed to maintain a neutral expression. When Hy finished making the sangria and passed him a replacement drink, Phil tasted it cautiously then, grateful, said, "Wendy, this is fabulous."

Everything was fabulous. For years afterwards, Phil would consider the small apartment his Platonic ideal and spend weeks at lease's end climbing badly-lit stairwells behind property managers, unable to articulate his desire beyond, "You know, a *pad.*" What he got shown, instead, was a series of dives, cramped rooms with no emotional resonance at all. With his time running out, he'd end up, desperately, settling on places that felt temporary from the time he took possession until the time he started searching again. One year he lived with a bedroom closet that opened to reveal the back of the refrigerator. He started freelancing for a couple of agencies then, and spent most of his time in the studio.

Wendy's own paintings, some familiar to him from

school, covered most of the wall space. The canvases were stretched but not framed, looking somehow more sincere as a result, but Phil was especially taken by the wall under the one double-hung window with its view of a similar window eight or ten feet away. Beneath that, the surface around the column radiator was lifted away in thick sheets, layers and layers of paint almost *authoritatively* cracked, like the bed of a dry lake. The impression was of a great force having thrust the matte-finish metal coils into the room from the outside. Bracketing the image were the first bean-bag chairs Phil had ever seen; shapeless, squooshy lumps covered with red, wet-look vinyl. Across from them, in the same fabric, a long, snake-like tube was folded back on itself twice, creating a deep, low-backed sofa.

Hy put the pitcher of sangria on a card table set with glasses, large plates of cut vegetables, and bowls of what appeared to be wet Plaster of Paris.

Phil pointed to the furniture, about to comment that he'd seen bean-bags in a magazine, but never in person. There was a knock at the door—*meat-on-the-hambone*—which took both Wendy and Hy from the room, so he was abandoned before indulging an impulse he later decided was unattractive: calling attention to details for which he has no responsibility. It's a passive way of calling attention to himself. It's a habit almost impossible for him to break, so instead he'll learn to be grateful for interruptions.

One of the first guests that Wendy introduces him to squeals, "Phil Peddles! I don't believe it. I just finished a year at *Cosmo*-girl school with your sister."

"Yes?" He didn't recognize her name. "I'll tell her we met."

"Oh, we weren't friends or anything. But I remember her. Everybody does and will forever. Right at the beginning of the year she got a hall pass. To go to the john?" She rolls her eyes. "The way secretaries have to do in offices, you know?" With one hand raised so her palm faces Phil, she says, "'Mr. Johnson, can I go pee-pee?'"

"Anyway, Alison wasn't gone for very long, and all of a sudden she bangs back into the room, holding up a tuna fish sandwich, and yells, 'This is my *brother's* lunch!'

"It was really surreal, almost *conceptual.* Do you have any idea what it meant?"

"Not a clue," Phil says quickly, starting to back away. "How could I? I wasn't there."

He intercepts Wendy as she's going to place another pitcher of sangria on the card table.

"I'm about due," he says.

A slice of lemon dams the spout as Wendy pours and she lifts it out, drops it into his glass.

"Don't count that as food," she says, putting down the pitcher and pointing to a tray where there's hacked-up broccoli ringed around a small bowl of dip. "You'd better eat something."

"I'm fine." Phil holds up his drink, the way the actors do in black-and-white movies. There's something he's supposed to add, a witty catch-phrase delivered with one eyebrow raised, but he can't think of anything.

"Men never eat vegetables, do they?" she asks. "Just

meat and potatoes, right? It's all meat and potatoes with you Georges. At least try the hummus."

Before Phil can respond, she's pulled the tips of two fingers through the bowl and is holding a rosette of dip up to his mouth.

Phil's scalp tightens. His skin is so taut over his skull that when he pulls his lips over his teeth, so they don't scrape Wendy's fingers, he thinks his head will burst. His forehead will split open in a line above his eyebrows and his entire blood supply will shoot out, all at once, like paint from a punctured spray can.

With his mouth slightly open, he nods and goes, "Uhmm, *humn,*" the sound mostly nasal, in the token noise meaning 'hot but delicious.' He doesn't wave his hand in front of his mouth, however, the dip being room temperature.

Hy leans into the space between them and says, "Donald wants to know where your guitar is."

"Tell him I gave it to my sister to take to camp," Wendy says and, when Hy goes to relay the message, she whispers to Phil, "It's really in the closet, but I don't want to hear *Kumbaya* again for the rest of my days. I'd better go make sure he has something else to do with his hands." She points back at the table. "Eat."

Phil looks down at the bowl of dip. He has no idea what it tasted like. He takes a deep swallow of his drink, on the chance that the new flavour will trigger a memory of the old. It doesn't seem to, so he tries again, then refills his glass.

At the party's maximum intensity, about a dozen people have the place heated up and Phil feels feverish. Nobody has expressed any surprise at his being there, or given any indication that he's only in on a pass. With some satisfaction, he notices that he's not the shortest man in the room. In the candlelight he might even look as old as everyone else. He moves from one pocket of conversation to the next, adeptly shifting gears, matching comments to topics. He's amazed at how helpful having read his mother's magazines proves to be; he always has something to contribute.

He knows that plush carpets tend to shed, and that shag needs to be raked. And he's able to suggest "Micro-fauna?" when a man loses his train of thought during a discussion of yoghurt's beneficial qualities. "But IUDs are not *contraception,*" he corrects one woman, his statement followed by a silence that sounds appreciative.

As the party winds down, he's standing with a cigarette in one hand, sangria in the other, and his back to the window.

"Far-out threads," a man tells him.

"Thanks."

"Where would you get something like that?"

"I sort of made it myself." Phil looks down at his chest. He can feel the radiator behind his calves, the cool metal coils. "I mean, it was a flag first, and then I made it."

"It's very..." The man puts his hand up to the vee of the neckline, taking the fabric between his fingers and thumb. His knuckles graze Phil's sternum. He extends his pinkie. "Very smooth," he says.

"Oh, well." Phil waves his cigarette in front of him,

almost under the man's nose. *"This,"* he says, by way of explanation or apology and twists away to stub it out. There's not quite enough room for the manoeuvre, not enough distance between them for Phil to keep both arms under control, although he's acutely aware of them. They're covered with goose bumps, the fine hairs standing on end. His drink tips and splashes over the bottom of the cape.

"Phil, come with me." Wendy appears at his side. "A little club soda will keep that from setting." She starts to pull him from the room, calling back, "Franklin, I think you'd better call me tomorrow. As soon as you get up, okay?"

Phil lets himself be drawn into the kitchen, where it's much brighter.

"It's all right," he says, watching her twist the cap off a bottle of club soda. The trapped carbon dioxide is released with a hiss. "I'm still having a good time."

"I'm glad." Wendy wrings out a sponge and pours soda over it. "Here," she says, and starts to blot at the flag, holding the fabric away from his waist. Her nails are cut short and straight across. "I'm a little surprised you're not at the dance."

"That's tonight?" Even to his own ears, his voice sounds false and evasive. "Yeah, it is," he admits. "I don't know, I didn't really want to go by myself."

"There wasn't anyone you wanted to ask?" She soaks the sponge and continues scrubbing at him, with more energy now. The dangling end of the chain belt jingles. "What about Margaret? I thought you two were pretty close."

"Oh, no," Phil says. By slow degrees, he pulls his hips

back, so he's pressed against the cabinet behind him. His palms are flat over the edge of the counter. "I mean, we're friends, but not like that."

"Yeah, I guess that's how it works. Girls that age never like the nice guys. Luckily, at least some of us grow out of it."

Phil's hands grip the counter edge. He runs what she's said through his mind. There's no ambiguity in the words, not that he can detect. She thinks he's a nice guy. She *likes* nice guys. And 'like' is, obviously, a euphemism.

"Damn!" Wendy abruptly pulls away from him. "Look what I've done. I'm really, really sorry."

"What?" Phil says. He glances down to where he can feel the damp cloth against his skin. The blue and red of the Union Jack have run into the white, creating a swirl of purple. He flaps the material up and down. "This is actually really cool. It's like tie-dye or batik or something."

"I just assumed it would be colour-fast." She drops the sponge into the sink. "Aren't they out in the wind and rain?"

"I guess this one's an indoor flag. Maybe that's why it was on sale in the first place. But I like it like this. Really, I do. I'm going to soak the whole thing, get it all to go like this."

"Well, thanks for reassuring me. Still, I ruined it, and I should make it up to you somehow."

"Hey, Wendy. Have you put down roots in there?" Hy sticks his head into the kitchen. "Peter and Carol are leaving."

"I'll be right there. Really," she adds, to Phil. "Let me know what I can do."

"Okay," he says. "Could I use your, uh . . ."

"Sure. Right through the bedroom." She points to the left, then goes to join Hy in the hall.

Phil listens to the social noises for a few seconds before he enters the next room, stopping just inside the door to get his bearings in the dimmer light. To take in the details. To gawk.

Wendy sleeps in a double bed. The mattress and box spring are right on the floor, covered with a paisley spread. Instead of a night table, there's a row of large art books, banded together and held upright by a man's leather belt, serving as a base for a sheet of glass, circular with a bevelled edge. The glass supports an old-fashioned black telephone and a clock-radio. In the glow of the lighted clock face, Phil can see that the radio is tuned to an FM station.

He walks lightly along the width of the bed to the bathroom, closing and locking the door behind him.

There's a lot of flapping and tugging before he gets things worked out. He slides the flag under the belt and bunches it up, keeps it out of the way by clamping it between his chin and his chest. The chain belt is warm against his naked belly. Done, he checks to make sure someone else has used one of the towels before he runs water over his hands, presses them into the already damp cloth.

On the back of the door is a full-length mirror in a painted frame, ivy vines against a white background. Phil stands in front of it and tries to re-drape the flag. He can't get the blousing quite the way it was, gives up, and puts the belt around his neck. He takes a step back to examine the effect. The patch where the colour has run is low down, close to the hem, a smudge of purple against the clean, hard-edged lines of red, white and blue. He can't get a complete picture of himself. His eyes keep returning to the patch. It's like a too-large signature painted on the lower, right-hand corner of a landscape. The material is the same, but the information is different.

He has his hand on the doorknob and is giving the room a quick, checking glance, when he spots a detail that had escaped him. In front of the tub, a deep, yellowing, enamelled thing on clawed feet, there is a small mat. Where a normal person might have a fluffy, rubber-backed square, where an *average* person would have a length of absorbent cotton, Wendy steps from the tub onto a white rabbit skin.

Phil bends down from the waist, keeping his legs straight, and examines the fur. He's not thinking of bunnies, how they change colour to camouflage themselves against the snow, not the shocking retort of gunshot on a clear and silent winter day. He's not thinking of the snapping jaws of a sprung trap, not the terrible squeal of helpless prey. He stretches out one hand and, lightly, puts the tips of his fingers into the depressions left by Wendy's toes. Warm and pink. Fresh from her bath.

In the bedroom, Phil looks closely at the table made of books, so he can pass on the information to his mother. He doesn't imagine she'll act on the tip—those big art books probably cost ten or fifteen dollars apiece—but she may be pleased to file it away with her other decorating 'ideas.'

The clock-radio makes a low, humming noise. Phil looks at the time, looks at the phone, weighing the possibility of

Alison answering if he calls home.

Back in the living room, Wendy is tearing off plastic wrap, covering the bowl and trays left on the card table. Hy is leaning against the wall beside her, with his arms crossed over his chest. Most of the candles have been snuffed. The overhead fixture is on.

"I haven't tried these yet," Phil says, flinging himself into one of the shiny red beanbags. The polystyrene pellets compact under his weight; there's a sound like a sigh. He lies on his side, pulls his knees up.

"A frog on a lily pad," Wendy says.

"Wait, wait." Phil is inspired. He stretches his legs out and hooks the other chair with his feet, slides it towards him. Then he half-pulls, half-lifts it on top of his body. "They're lips," he explains, although he thinks this must be obvious. "It's a mouth."

"And what are you supposed to be?" Hy asks. "The tongue?"

Phil and Wendy exchange a look. Her glasses catch the ceiling light. Even the plastic wrap stretched over the bowl in her hands glows with reflected light like a tiny moon.

"Of course not," Phil says, curbing the archness that threatens his civil tone: not everyone appreciates Art. He flings out one arm. "I'm *lunch.*"

"Well, gosh," Hy says. "Look at the time. So, how are you planning to get home?"

"Oh, I missed the last bus half-an-hour ago." Phil has a small struggle, getting the top beanbag off, and sort of claws himself into a sitting position. "But it's all right. I don't have to get home." He looks in Wendy's direction, without looking at her face. "I borrowed your phone. They're not expecting me."

"I—Hy, give me a hand with these, okay?" Wendy starts passing him trays and bowls, the lot precariously stacked to clear the table in one trip, making what Phil's mother would call 'a lazy man's load.'

"Right back," she says, giving Phil a broad smile. He dips his head, managing not to wink. Not while Hy's in the room. He's not insensitive.

Alone, he stands and fluffs up the beanbags, enjoying the way they resist a bit before giving under his hands. The sensation is like smoothing a place in the sand to stretch out on the beach. He can hear Wendy and Hy in the kitchen, their voices low and overlapping. Phil imagines she's giving Hy his walking papers. He hopes there's not going to be a scene.

He's relieved at how amicable they appear when they come back into the room.

"I was going to make coffee," Wendy says. "But I'm all out, not even instant. So I thought we could go to Harvey's."

In the back seat of Hy's Vauxhall, leaning forward with his elbows on the tops of the driver's and passenger's seats, Phil watches the city come at him through the windshield. He wonders if he should have pointed out, back at the apartment, that they were only three or four blocks from the Party Palace. It wasn't really necessary to get in the car and drive clear across town. They're practically in his neighbourhood now, going down Baseline Road, past the car dealerships, the GEM store, a skeleton of a garden-home row, the expansive fields of the Experimental Farm, knee-high in corn.

There's a fresh-scrubbed look to the street at this hour, a reflective cast. Everything is hard-edged and clear under the streetlights. Phil has never been here at this hour before. It's as new and strange to him as Addis Ababa would be. He can't think of anything to say, and doesn't disturb the silence in the car.

"Here we are," Hy says, pulling into the Harvey's parking lot. He turns his head and says, "Why don't you get the coffee?"

"We're not going in?" Phil climbs out of the car, bends to lean into Wendy's window. "Okay, I'll do it. What do we want?"

"Just black for us," Wendy says. "Hy, give him the money."

"Forget it," Phil says. "I've got money." He takes out his wallet, to prove this, and he has it in his hand when he steps up to the counter. He's the only customer there and, for some reason, he almost whispers his order.

"Two black, one double-double."

"You sure?" The girl points over his shoulder.

Phil stares at her hand for a moment, the way a dog does when it's told, "Look!" Her skin looks blue in the fluorescent light, waxy and unreal. He has to tug his attention back, then he turns to see what she means. The Vauxhall is pulling out of the parking lot. Neither Wendy nor Hy look back. They might be test-crash dummies, the way they're sitting, rigidly upright, staring straight ahead.

"I drink a *lot* of coffee," Phil says, turning back to the girl.

He carries the three paper cups out to the parking lot and sits at the picnic table there, instead of sitting at a booth inside. By taking a large mouthful of each of the burnt-tasting, harsh, black coffees, he makes enough room to dilute the rest with his own. His last six cigarettes are crushed from being carried tucked into the waistband of his jeans, but only one has the paper split. He straightens out the rest and smokes slowly, sipping at his coffee, until the orange-and-white Harvey's sign goes out with an electric crackle. This is his cue to leave, before the girl comes out. He pulls himself to his feet, dropping the last butt-end into a half-full cup. He's emptied two; she won't think he was lying about his appetite, if she checks.

Once he leaves the road, cutting diagonally across fields that were once farms, he might be the only man in the world. Behind him, the streetlights recede to a thin line on the horizon, a faint glow like sunrise. And then there are lights ahead of him, as his neighbourhood nears.

His shoes and the cuffs of his jeans are soaked with dew. He stands inside the door of his building. He can't go upstairs. He never did call, to tell his mother he was staying out. It's too late to explain anything now.

He doesn't have a key. Even if he could somehow pick the lock and let himself in, he'd have to turn on the lights, in case she's moved the furniture. He could break a leg, trying to navigate by memory.

He goes downstairs. The laundry room is unlocked. There's a piece of folded linoleum, used to hold the door open in the daytime, that he wedges under the door from the inside. He stands in front of the stationery tub and empties his bladder, faster than the drain can take it away, creating a swirling whirlpool, flowing counter-clockwise. His knees twitch with relief. In seven weeks he'll turn sixteen and, a few months after that, he'll get his driver's licence. For a time, he'll be feverish with possibility, the feeling that he can go *anywhere,* pack up and split. This will be followed by a jolt of crushing reality. Without a car, he's as grounded as he ever was. The licence was only a formality, a ticket rather than transportation.

He gets down on the floor and crawls under the stationery tub. There's not enough room to stretch out, but it seems important that he be tucked-in, not out in the open. He hooks his feet around the metal struts supporting the tub, anchoring him in place, so he doesn't roll away. The poured concrete over his head has an odour like disinfectant. He puts his hand up, above his face, but the tub hasn't been at all warmed by the hot stream from his body. The floor is also cool, and as hard. Only because he's exhausted is he able to fall asleep, wrapped in the flag of another country.

A GLASS ANNIVERSARY

Across the street, in the park, a man in very small lavender satin shorts and rubber flip-flops is pushing a child in a stroller along the sidewalk. A dog lopes into view from behind some trees to the right, and bounds towards them. Its front and back paws are not in a straight line but almost perpendicular to its spine, like the hounds in a Colville painting.

"Something's about to happen," Dave says. He's twenty years old; anticipation is a natural state for him. Most things have yet to happen.

"Where?" Gail lifts her head from the blanket she's spread over the grass on her front lawn, and pulls off her sunglasses, bright green plastic with almost black lenses. The shoulder straps of her white one-piece bathing suit are pushed down, trapping her upper arms against her body. From a distance, she'd look like she was naked, evening up the tan of her arms and legs, her back. She's taking a week off work; her kids are still in school, her husband, Richard, is at his office.

"There." Dave angles his head instead of pointing.

"The guy in the shorts?" She squints, puts her glasses back on. "And the kid?"

"Man sees daughter eaten by dog. I can't look," he says, turning back to face the park. The man is standing beside the stroller, holding one of the child's hands in his own, and he's patting the dog in long, even strokes. The child's body looks like it's been peeled away from the white canvas stroller, pliant and boneless. The dog acts pleased, wagging its tail so its whole body jiggles. It's a thin, spotted animal.

"He's introducing them. I don't believe it."

"He's a dad," Gail says. "That's his job."

"Really, a dad?" Dave laughs. He likes Gail's categories for people, her easy reductions. He's noticed, especially, how she talks about marriage as a thing 'apart,' that has its own internal logic, seemingly arbitrary rules to be ignored at one's own peril. "It's not two people with a single heart beating," she says. "It's more like a corporate entity. You have to work for it. There's nothing you can take for granted." When she uses the word *divorce* she says it with the same tone Dave has heard some people say *cancer,* suggesting distance from an inevitable occurrence in the lives of others.

Gail has been married since college, when she quit during first year to work putting Richard though graduate school. Then there were the early, low-rung-on-the-career-ladder jobs, fitting the two kids into sick leave and vacation days. Dave's never met Richard, but he imagines someone like a pilot in an airline commercial, efficient and stable.

"And do we like dads?" he asks.

"Nice ones, we do."

She turns to lie on her back and reaches for the plastic bottle of water she uses to splash her skin when it gets too hot from the sun. He passes it over. Supine, she snaps the bottle in his direction, squeezing the soft sides. Cold water slops over his T-shirt; the skin on his arms ripples into duck flesh. He makes a sound like *whumph.*

"Look at this." He holds out one forearm. "A systemic wimp. Betrayed by my own skin."

"Skin's an organ," she says. "Not a system."

"My shirt's soaked." He pulls a tent of the light blue cotton away from his chest.

"It'll dry."

Dave brings his knees up to his chest, crosses his arms over them and supports his head on the X of his wrists. He should get home, pick up something to eat on the way. He has two term papers to finish, before his exams.

Spring is early this year. Downtown, in the shadows of the tallest buildings, there are still patches of snow, rough and pebbly from melting and re-freezing, but under him, the grass is warm and dry. Solid ground, people say, although not so long ago, there had been a rumble through the land, when a nuclear power plant in Harrisburg came close to melt down. How close is anyone's guess. It had potential to be an international incident; accidents on that scale are handled as government secrets. Any information released now is suspect, just politics.

Dave worked for a minor politician, his first summer job, two years ago. His day consisted almost entirely of personalizing form letters to immigrants.

Dear Quann Family, *Welcome to Canada. I sincerely hope you are enjoying your new home at* 5002 Cumberland. . . . *Remember to vote . . .*

He worked quietly, pacing himself, and thought he was unnoticed. When the research assistant told him he was wanted in the minister's office, her expression unreadable, he flashed back, viscerally, as if being summoned to the principal's office. Room 101.

"Sir?" Dave stood on the carpet just inside the office door. "You wanted to see me?"

"Yes. It's, uhm, Dave?" The minister stood up and walked around the five or six yards of polished desk that separated them. "I was hoping you could give me a hand."

"A hand?"

"You see, uhm, Dave?" The minister spoke as though there were more than two people in the room, his voice projected to the far corners, to the rafters. "My wife hasn't been well lately."

"I'm sorry to hear it." Dave, with some effort, kept his hands out the pockets of his grey flannel trousers.

"Oh, that's not the problem." The man made a wide, dismissive gesture with his left arm. "The problem is that she hasn't been able to get out to buy me some new shirts. And the one I have on now seems to have come back from the laundry a little small."

"Yes?" Dave's own shirt, from a distance, would appear to be lightly spotted. Closer up, the spots were tiny printed chickens. An exchange would be incongruous. The man was also twice his size.

"If you could give me a hand with this?" The minister pulled the knot of his tie down to mid-chest, stepped towards Dave and lifted his chin to expose a smoothly-shaven neck with a gap of at least an inch between the collar's button and buttonhole. "To do it up."

Dave moved forward, into an enveloping cloud of bar soap and baby powder, damp wool, taking hold of the two sides of the collar.

"I can try," he said, without conviction. The man turned his head, tipped back so the whites of his eyes showed. Dave brought his hands together.

"Ark."

"Sorry." Dave released his hold. "I'm not sure I can do it this way. Maybe if I stood behind you, it'd be like doing up my own."

They shuffled around each other until Dave was in a position to reach over the man's shoulders. He put his knee between the man's legs for leverage and, eyes closed, tried to imagine he was doing up his own collar.

"Ark."

"Don't *fidget,*" Dave snapped, forgetting himself in his concentration. "Just keep still." He dropped his head to the heavily-padded shoulder of the man's suit and tried again. The minister pulled away and turned to face him.

"Look, I think it'll be okay. I can run out at lunch and pick up some new shirts. Maybe I've put on weight."

"Well, if you're sure," Dave said, trying not to stare at the man's neck. There were two thumb-sized marks, changing from white to dull heliotrope, that would become bruises, on the neck of an elected representative. The one with the wife who wasn't well.

It was a little after eleven when the research assistant stood in front of Dave's typewriter and said, "Get your jacket and come with me."

Dave turned off his machine, folded his blazer over his arm, and followed her to the elevators.

"You realize you gave that man a hickey?" she said. "Or, more importantly, that's what people will think."

Dave stared for a moment at the Down button. He took a breath and thought of the phrase 'playing in the major leagues.' Looking slightly past her, to a distant future, he asked, "Does this mean I'm fired?"

"Fired?" She laughed, way too loud for the marbled corridor they were in. "Christ, no. I'm taking you to lunch. Oh," she added, "I'm Gail."

Dave's apartment is on the third floor of a house six blocks from where Gail and Richard live, but it might as well be in another city, that's how different the neighbourhoods are. His bedroom looks out at a twenty-four-hour-bread-and-milk place. He hardly needs the room's overhead fixture; car headlights sweep the ceiling almost all night long. The hardwood floors are worn smooth in the centres of the two rooms, to the colour of beaten egg. Where previous tenants had furniture pushed to the wall, there are rough borders, dark with oily stains that have resisted turpentine, steel wool, even a butter knife. The kitchen and bathroom floors are tiled in hexagons not much larger than quarters. After drying off from a shower, Dave sits on the edge of the tub and pulls loose tiles from the soles of his feet, fits them back into their spaces. He hardly uses the kitchen, just for morning coffee, mostly, or reheating take-out pizza.

He is deeply 'at home' here. It's his first place on his own, and he's acquiring the accoutrements of the newly-independent: a red, touchtone Contempra phone, a goose-neck lamp with an enamelled goose-head shade, subscriptions to *Psychology Today, Esquire, Macleans.*

"What was that noise?" he asks the closed bathroom door. "Are you looking in my medicine cabinet?"

"For sure," through the door. "A classic case."

"What? What's classic?"

Gail opens the door, leaves the bathroom. One step takes her into the living room. "Nothing," she says. "I was just getting you going. But you really do use a lot of stuff for your hair and face. Aftershave skin renewal?"

"I try to take care of myself," Dave says. "It's not like make-up or anything. I suppose Richard slaps on some cold water and shaves with a steak knife?"

"He has an electric. When you're married, with kids, those things aren't really a priority." She runs her palm over the parsons-style table holding Dave's typewriter, library books with torn strips of paper marking the places he'll quote in his essay, a ceramic mug. She hasn't been in the apartment before; they usually meet at the restaurant.

Dave opens the single closet door, then decides against

wearing a jacket. He pats his pockets, checking for wallet and keys.

"This isn't a bad place, for what you're paying. Our first apartment was over a mortuary. Real depressing. But we managed to save enough for the down payment on the house."

"I like it."

She crosses to where Dave has a framed mirror on the wall, narrows her eyes, steps back from her image.

"You know about these things," she says. "Do you think my hair is scuzzy? Should I try to do something with it?"

"Wouldn't hurt," Dave says. "Nobody rolls out of bed in the morning looking like people in magazines."

"Wrong answer," she says. "You pay for lunch."

The Modern Cafe has been in operation practically since the city's founding, one of those businesses that survives by making no concessions at all to its customers, establishing itself as a habit sheerly by being familiar, without surprises.

After Gail first took Dave there, they started having lunch together on paydays, taking turns treating. That first day, he'd been apologetic, talking too quickly about his plans for the fall. He had wanted to establish himself as competent, forward-thinking.

"I'm not a stupid person," he said. "Sometimes I make mistakes."

"I wouldn't want to work with anyone who'd take pride in that job. You'd have to be brain-dead to keep your mind on anything so inane."

"But I felt stupid," Dave said. "I've never tried to dress anyone before. I really don't like being made to feel foolish."

"It was funny." Gail laughed. "The look on his face. Anyway, I had a good time, so lunch is on me."

"This is my reward?" Dave looked around, calculating.

The restaurant is divided in two by a series of arches, with a bright mural that looks crayoned on the surrounding stucco wall. A jovial shepherdess, red-cheeked and thick-lipped, dominates the foreground, with a bust that shelves out in a restatement of the terraced hills behind her. Goats gambol over the hills. By a trick of perspective they range in comparative sizes, from that of a small dog to an eighteen-wheel diesel truck.

On one side there are tables and chairs with a remarkable similarity to the chrome dinette sets in a 50s department store catalogue. The population of this side, apparently, feels comfortable with the furnishings. Dave, feeling crass, assumes they go home to much the same decor. If they go home at all. He's seen through the window, when he was walking home from work, the same people from lunchtime, sitting around a table surfaced with empty draught glasses, cigarette packs, overflowing ashtrays, crumpled paper napkins.

The other side, where Dave and Gail sit, is more formal, with cloth table linens, water glasses, and the draught is served in pub-style mugs. But the food is the same on both sides, what Dave thinks of as 'Canadian cuisine.'

"I'm having the barbecued chicken burger," he says. It's what he always has. On the menu, this is *Bar-B-Q*. "Why don't you have a toasted cheese sandwich?"

"Because you're paying? No way." Gail passes her menu to the waitress. "I'll have the deep-fried shrimp."

"Shrimp inna basket," the waitress says. "Anything to drink?" She's an older woman, wearing white Wallabees with her uniform, a shapeless burgundy shift of glassy-looking fabric. Dave has a weakness, nostalgic rather than patronizing, for matronly waitresses, the type who might at any moment call him 'Hon' or 'Dear.'

"Draught for me," Dave says. He looks across the table. "And a glass of white wine?" Gail nods. The waitress walks away, looking down at her shoes. The backs of her legs appear grey through her thick stockings.

"Richard's going to Amsterdam." This is delivered like a sentence from the middle of a paragraph, and Dave turns the side of his head, his ear, to Gail, meaning for her to repeat this.

"There's a conference," she says. "And Richard is taking off in ten days. I spent all of yesterday on the phone, changing plans we'd already made."

"Well, it's his job, after all," Dave says. He thinks ten days is a lot of time, and he's been told that Richard is a world-class economist. Reasonably, there is no crisis, nothing has happened that couldn't be expected. "You couldn't go with him?"

"With two kids? Forget it. It's just so inconsiderate of him, to leave now." She shakes her head. "I don't even want to talk about it. So, how're you doing?"

"I'm up to my hips in dead Jews," Dave says. The food and drinks arrive at this moment, and he hurries to explain in case the comment, overheard, was insensitive. "My history paper on the Warsaw ghetto. It's the most depressing research I've ever done."

While they eat, he tells her what he's learning, about the creation of the *Judenrat,* ostensibly a democratic Jewish organization, like the Council of Elders, headed by Adam Czerniakow.

"In fact, the first meeting was held in the presence of a Gestapo officer named Mende. This was in 1939. Can you imagine what that must have felt like? That kind of absolute powerlessness." Dave puts his knife and fork down over his plate, handles to the right. "Then I have this psychology course where I'm supposed to believe that taking responsibility for my own life is the path to mental health. I know I'm at school to be broadened, but I think I'm being stretched awfully thin."

"You've certainly given me something to think about," Gail says. "I guess there's an inevitable alienation between military organizations and political leadership. It's probably more about male egos than anything else."

"Maybe it was all personal? Good point. I wonder if I can use it?"

She crumples her napkin and puts it in the wicker basket now emptied of shrimp, then rests her chin in one palm.

"If I buy whatever you put on your hair, would you come back to my place and show me how to use it?"

"Thank you, a lot." Dave takes the drink and holds it in his lap. The jeans he has on are worn thin and soft; he can feel the cold glass through the fabric. He crosses his legs to create a more secure pocket. If he stood up, he would come maybe to Richard's eyebrows. The man is well over six feet tall, dark-haired, with spaniel-brown eyes that have only a narrow edge of white. He's taken off his suit jacket, and stands in front of Dave in a shirt and tie, belted trousers.

"So, how long is she going to take?" Richard asks. He looks up at the ceiling, through which can be heard the sound of the running shower.

"She just has to rinse her hair," Dave says.

Gail's kids had come home from school after she'd changed into a white terrycloth robe and wet down her hair at the sink. She had been sitting on one of the kitchen chairs pulled into the middle of the room while Dave worked a deep-treatment conditioner through her hair. He had had a dishtowel, printed with a giant panda, tucked into his shirt collar. The kids, Mark and Jenny, had stood watching, rolling their shoulders over the lower cabinets. Their eyes were milky blue, as if they had cataracts, the eyes of old people. Dave, inspired, had shaped Gail's hair into a single, thick horn rising from the top of her head.

"What's your mother look like now?" he had asked. He was thinking of a unicorn.

"An ice-cream cone," Jenny had said, thrusting three fingers into her mouth, to contain herself.

"Pebbles Flintstone," Mark shrieked.

Dave had laughed and bent over to look at Gail face-on, then straightened when he saw Richard. He had tugged down the dishtowel, holding it limp at his side. He had felt a sense of inappropriateness, the way he might have felt if he had turned off a radio that was playing a John Lennon song: it just wasn't done.

"What's this?" Richard had said as he swung his attache case onto the counter. Its black plastic handle clicked against the metal reinforcement band between the locks. He had clapped his hands. "Kids, up to your rooms."

Then Gail stood up, pulled the belt of her bathrobe tight, and made the introductions.

"Am I about done?" she had asked Dave. He nodded, and she went upstairs, with the kids.

Richard scraped the chair back under the table, offered Dave a drink, and led the way through the dining room.

"Well?" Richard looks down.

Dave follows his gaze, says, "Oh, yes," and lifts his glass, sips the drink.

"It's single malt." Richard holds the rim of his glass with the tips of his fingers, his elbows held away from his body, so he brings his mouth to the drink, rather than the reverse, and takes a deep swallow.

"It's very nice." Dave moves his hand up from the base of his own glass, which he's been clutching like a weight for arm-curls, drinks again. He tips his head to the side, thoughtful. After a moment he says, "No burn."

"A civilized drink for a man."

"You're being civilized? That's good." Gail comes into the living room. She's put on a red sweater and white slacks, and has a towel wrapped like a turban around her head. Her feet are bare.

"You were expecting us to be duking it out?" Richard asks. He brings his drink hand into his chest, raises his other hand, fisted. "Put 'em up, boy."

"Some men might be a little upset to come home and find their wives in their nightclothes with a strange man," Gail says. She stands beside Richard and puts her arm around his waist. "I don't give you enough credit for not being like that. Anyway, you know about Dave. He's an old friend, from work."

"Just that summer. I'm at school now," Dave explains. "We were having lunch."

This passes without remark. Gail and Richard seem to have forgotten he's here. He looks past them, out the window. There's a child on a tricycle in the middle of the street, pedalling in narrowing circles. Beyond that, the park grass is darkening in patches as the sun dips below the level of the trees. Dave considers gulping the rest of his drink, or leaving it on the table beside him, but he's not sure what single malt means. It could be something really expensive, or very sophisticated; he doesn't want to be unappreciative or boorish.

He checks the level of his glass, glances up, and sees Richard look at him over the top of Gail's towelled head.

"Will she have beautiful hair for Wednesday night?" he asks.

"I guess." Dave shrugs. "You could do it again, before that. Why?"

"Her big night," Richard says. "Isn't that what this is about?"

"Richard," Gail says. "Never mind, Dave."

"No, I should apologize. I'm sorry, Dave, that you had to move heaven and earth with your social calendar to accommodate my job. It was inconsiderate of me."

Dave puts his glass down. He rubs his hands on his jeans before he stands. "I should be going." Nobody moves or speaks, so he adds, "I'm confused. Did I say something?"

"It's our anniversary party," Gail says. "It was supposed to be the week Richard's going to be away. I've had to move it up."

"Amsterdam. I remember."

"Wait," Richard says. "You weren't invited? Have I put my foot in it?"

They've started, the three of them, moving towards the house's front door, the way people move towards the box office of a theatre when they've arrived in plenty of time, momentarily relieved of purpose.

"It's all older people. I'm sure you understand." Gail unwraps the towel from her hair as Dave pushes open the door to the porch. "I didn't think you'd be comfortable."

"Older people?" Richard repeats. "We're already older people? I hope that's not true."

"Well, couples, then," Gail says.

"Oh, couples. Yes."

"Hey," Dave says. "That's okay. I'll be about in the middle of exams then. Really busy. But call me for lunch, after."

He stands on the porch, in the cooling air, and pushes the

screen door closed. Richard has one arm against the top of the inside frame. Gail holds the towel in front of her. They become silhouettes through the fine mesh, lit from behind by the kitchen light at the end of the hall. Dave squints at the disappearance of details.

"Gail," he nods. "Richard."

Dave holds up his hands, with his fingers spread, and looks closely at his cuticles. He makes a fist, and scrapes his thumbnail against a front tooth. He pushes back his chair from the table and stretches, then tucks his shirt back into his jeans. Yawning, he stands and goes into the kitchen, to check the clock on the stove panel. This is labelled Time Control Centre. He's never noticed that before. He rubs his eyes with the heels of his hands. Maybe, if he set back the clock, he'd be able to finish his term paper before the exam Thursday. Later today, actually. It's one-fifteen. Time control, there's a concept.

He goes back to his place in front of the typewriter. The top third of the paper is dense with statistics: the number of tons of sugar and flour delivered to the Warsaw ghetto, the death toll from typhoid and cholera. The Jews have decided on a policy of non-resistance, convinced the Nazis will deport only sixty thousand of their number, not hundreds of thousands.

Dave rolls in a new sheet of paper, types *Rumours of the reality of the 'resettlement actions' reached Czerniakow and he had First, a member of the Jewish Council, check the stories with Security Police officers.*

He laces his fingers together, cracks his knuckles. There is no conclusion to this essay, no moral he can draw, no final statement on . . . *the corrosive effect of victimization.* His door buzzer sounds. He scratches the top of his thigh, then realizes *door buzzer,* what that means, and he gets up to open the door.

A man, carrying a paper bag, is coming up the stairwell. Dave can see only the top of his head, wondering who it might be, until the man turns on the landing.

"Richard?" He steps back into his apartment, leaving the door open so the short hall has better light.

"Dave. Can I come in?" Richard moves past him and pushes the door closed. His breathing is audible. The suit he's wearing is rumpled. There is a rust-coloured spot where the outside trouser seam meets the pocket. "I brought a gift for the host." He pulls a bottle out of the bag. "Or am I the host? I didn't think you should miss all of Gail's little party."

"Well," Dave says. "That's nice. I'm—" He points at the typewriter, the books stacked on the table around it.

"Don't be so serious. It's not healthy." Richard is in the kitchen; it's not much more than an open closet off the living room. He tugs at the cupboards and takes down two water tumblers. "Ice?" He disappears behind the refrigerator door. There's a sound like loose change emptied from pockets, at bedtime, dropping on the surface of a dresser. "Did you know glass is traditional for a fifteenth anniversary? So, you can't not have a glass of scotch with me. Can't argue with tradition."

"Okay." Dave accepts the glass.

He looks around the room, then turns the chair away from the typewriter, sits on the edge. Richard carries the bottle of scotch with him, puts it on the floor beside the couch, then leans back against the cushions. His drink is cupped in both hands between his legs. He's tall enough that his knees are pushed up, higher than his waist. He lolls his head back.

Dave gulps half his scotch, quickly, before Richard looks up. Single malt. No burn.

"How's Gail?"

"Gail? She's fine." He leans forward, as if he's falling, then puts one hand down to the floor, grasps the bottle and re-fills his glass. "Her hair looked wonderful." Richard laughs, suddenly, his face flushing. "Stunning," he says. "Divine." He puts the bottle down, hard, and Dave wonders if this could be heard through the floor. The woman downstairs is a nurse and works shifts.

"Good." Dave takes another swallow of scotch, puts the almost-empty glass on the table at his side. The edge of his hand leaves a mark on the wood, a damp crescent quickly shrinking into its centre. "Thanks for the drink," he says. "I really should get back to work."

He starts to stand. Richard waves him down.

"Don't spoil the party. God, you're a sober young man. These are supposed to be the best years of your life. Learn to enjoy." Richard narrows his eyes. "Just how old are you, anyway?"

"Me? Twenty." Dave slumps back in the chair. "Listen,

are you sure you should be here?"

"Twenty," Richard says. He cocks his head and looks reflective. "I was never twenty. I *turned* twenty, maybe, but I never got to *be* twenty. I don't know, she might have been right. Start early, make a commitment." He glances up, at a point past Dave. His eyes are too bright to be focused. "Are they still saving it?" he asks. "Or are they just making you pay for it?" He purses his lips and makes a sound, the way someone might try to coax an unnamed kitten to come out from under the sofa: *tch, tch, tch.*

"This is not a conversation I want to have." Dave carries his glass into the kitchen, leans against the counter there.

"Come on, you're a student. We can keep it academic."

"I don't think so," Dave starts. He falls silent as Richard's head drops down to his chest. The hand holding his drink tips forward on the arm of the couch, but nothing spills.

"Richard?" he whispers. "Richard?"

There's no answer. He sighs, then moves to take a blanket from the closet. The glass is easily pulled from Richard's limp hand. He puts it on the floor, beside the bottle of scotch, then flips the blanket over Richard's chest, so he looks like he's in a barber's chair. He's about to kneel and pull off the man's shoes, when Richard shifts his weight, sliding down.

"I could have gone," he mumbles. "I could have been at Woodstock."

"Yeah," Dave says, standing. "I guess you could have."

He turns off the overhead on the way out of the room,

uses the toilet, then pulls off his own clothes, down to his briefs, and climbs into bed. A car's headlights whiten the ceiling in a broad arc, then vanish. He closes his eyes.

He's trying out for his high school's track team. His shoes are soled with tiny rubber suction cups, like the tentacles of an octopus. These are arranged in fingerprint whorls. The starter pistol explodes in the fresh spring air. Dave pushes off from the block, his weight coming down neatly on the left foot, heel and toe. When he tries to lift off, he's trapped. His sole is gripping the track. In the grassy oval the track surrounds, there's a man wearing a dark, narrow suit and a tall hat. The air lifts the sidecurls from his cheeks. "Run," he shouts. "Run with the others. This is not a practice. If you don't run, you die." Reserves of strength return to him. He takes a deep breath and twists his upper body.

He open his eyes. Richard is kneeling on the bed beside him. He has the sheet thrown back, and he's dragging Dave across the mattress, towards him. His hands are warm on Dave's legs, as he works his fingers between his thighs.

"What?" Dave kicks out, a reflex, and pushes himself up, into a sitting position. "Stop," he says. "Just stop."

Richard crawls off the bed, his weight on his hands, and stands up. He's in stocking feet. His shirt is unbuttoned, although his tie is still knotted in a pinched width of striped fabric. The light from the window is pale blue, like the light from a television seen through a window. The curtains that came with the apartment have a ragged and water-stained lining. Dave is afraid to tug them closed; they might come apart in his hands.

"Relax," Richard says. "I just wanted to see if it would have been worth it."

"Go." Dave points to the door of the room. The skin of his arm is the same colour as the veins inside his elbow. He stretches his lips back from his teeth. "Now."

He waits, hearing bumping sounds from the next room, short whispers, the clink of glass, and, finally, heavy footsteps on the stairs down to the door of the building. He listens, but doesn't hear a car start up. All the digits on the clock radio flip over. It's five o'clock.

He gets out of bed, wrapping the sheet around his body, slams the door, and walks into the living room. It looks shabby in this light, as though no one has lived here for some time.

The last page of his essay is still in the typewriter. He glances over what he has written, then turns the chair around and sits down. He types *The rumours were true. Treblinka was in operation. On July 22, 1942, the 'resettlement' began. On this day, Adam Czerniakow committed suicide.*

Dave reads this out loud, shaking his head. He pushes the return bar, twice, then adds his name and student number. There's nothing else he can do.

It was in the newspaper. The Modern Cafe, a fixture since 1946, is going to be torn down to make way for a fourteen-story office building. City planning committees have approved the demolition, and construction should start early next spring.

"It's the end of an era," Dave says. "Did you see that the

chicken burger used to be less than fifty cents?" He cuts into his, forks up chicken, roll, and sauce together.

"I read that, yes," Gail says. "The article didn't make adjustments for the cost of living though. That fifty cents had a lot of buying power."

"I never know what to make of those comparisons, when they're made," Dave says. "I don't think you can tote up individual prices and come up with the cost of your life. Or its value."

"No? Richard does. That's his job." Gail takes a sip of wine. "Did I tell you what he got me for our anniversary?" She opens her suede shoulderbag, propping it against the corner of the table. She fishes inside for a moment, then hands him a slim plastic machine.

"A solar calculator?" Dave tips the calculator so the four collector cells dully reflect the room's light. He laughs. "I guess it is a *little* more romantic than a new hose for the vacuum cleaner."

"No, it's what I wanted. He's not insensitive," Gail says. "You know what he said? He said he thinks we're having an affair. Not a real one, sort of intellectual."

"Platonic." Dave swallows. The barbecue sauce has a metallic, artificial taste. It's very red on the plate. "And I guess he doesn't want you getting involved in my life. I understand. I mean, he's your husband, after all. Wouldn't want to mess with that. He's a big man. Besides, he knows where I live."

There's a sound, first, and then a spreading dampness. Dave looks down at his lap, where the broken glass is spilling wine over the napkin spread there. His shirt is spotted. He looks up, and Gail is out of her chair, leaning over the table. He puts his hand over the shank of his fork. Then she turns, and leaves. The shoulderbag she has clutched in one fist swings furiously.

Dave folds the corners of the napkin over the shards of glass, then puts it on the table beside his plate. It makes a fragile, tinkling sound. The waitress comes over to the table.

"You've had a little accident? Should I get you another glass?" she asks.

"I don't think my friend will be back."

The woman bends closer to him, confidingly. "Would you like a little more sauce for your chicken? I could run your plate back into the kitchen."

"I don't think so." Dave looks at the table. The white bun and chunks of chicken are stained with sauce. The coleslaw, on the side of the plate, looks like shredded newsprint. "But I'll have another draught. No, a scotch. Single malt. Wait. A draught *and* a scotch."

"See them?" The waitress points through the arches, to a group of people at a large table with no plates or cutlery, only glasses. The men are large, coarse-looking, with the high colour of *essential hyper-tension*; the women are drab, bleached like old photographs too long tucked into the frame around a mirror.

"I've seen them before," Dave says.

"That's okay for them, but I can tell you're not like that. You don't want another drink."

"What? I'm not? No, no, I guess I'm not like that." He

looks up at the woman. She has a lace-edged handkerchief neatly folded and pinned to her uniform, where a man's shirt would have a pocket. Embroidered in the centre of this, spidery lettering spells out *Audrey.* It's not a common name, not any more.

"My friend?" he says. "The one who left? It was her turn to pay."

OPTIONS

You find her, mostly, in the places you'd expect. Fortyish, she's too young yet to lighten her hair, and naturally too fair to go darker. She's slightly over-dressed, even at a fund raiser for the opera, in a beaded suit more appropriate for an opening act in Vegas. At a gallery exhibition for an already well-known artist (nothing under five thousand), her white blouse will be dotted with seed pearls, her black velvet skirt trimmed with sequins. The effect is subtly trashy.

But she's not cheap. On these occasions, which she calls "functions," she has one drink, whatever is clear: bottled water, white wine, vodka-tonic. One. Nobody has seen her leave half-way through a reception at the club, as others have, wandering through the parking lot to find an unlocked car, sitting inside with her make-up running, tiny flecks of mascara settling into the lines around her eyes. Being in that position would be unthinkable. She has a reputation, she would say.

She uses her maiden name because more people have heard of her father than her husband.

Oil had dropped to six dollars a barrel, research into alternative energy sources was losing support, and Alex Brinkholder's tar-sands options were almost worthless.

"It can't last," he said. "Not more than a couple of years. I've got to have the liquidity to renew. This is no time to be short-sighted."

"There's nothing more short-sighted than touching capital," Eleanor said, meaning her own, the trust left to her by her parents. "Maybe you should cut your losses and move on to something else?"

"Like what? What else can I move on to now? We agreed on this, dammit, back when I put everything into those options. We have to hang on to them. People are going to be begging for new energy sources. It's only a matter of time before they'll be enough to put me back on top. Those options are our future."

Constance skirted the living room and carried her books upstairs. She recognized the tone of her parents' voices; they would be circling the topic for the rest of the evening, never once mentioning the word *money.* Dinner would be delayed while her father lingered over "one last drink," two or three fingers of scotch, topped up with decreasingly stealthy trips to the mahogany cabinet.

In the kitchen, Eleanor would prop open a cookbook on the counter, pull over a chair from the breakfast set, and take discreet sips from a gin-and-tonic before deciding to run cold water over whatever was left in the freezer. By the time whatever she found was thawed and prepared—usually a block of fish, overcooked and too-heavily salted—Constance would have as little appetite as her parents.

After a suitable interval had passed and the table was cleared, Constance would run more cold water over the left-over food, to wash off the salt before offering the fish to the cat, Agatha.

Up in her room at the front of the house, Constance shed her school uniform. The woollen jumper was slipped onto a padded hanger, under the jacket, necktie folded over one shoulder, blouse and socks dropped into the hamper.

She changed into a tight denim skirt and a man's tattersall shirt. Her reflection in the mirror on the inside of the closet door showed an untroubled young woman, clear-eyed and shiny with good health. She was seventeen.

Years later a man leaned into her at a reception for the Museum of Fine Arts and shared his observation that all the young women attending the high school he passed on the way to work appeared cheap.

"It's something about the hair, the mousse or gel, it looks dirty. And the clothes are a bit hookerish."

The man looked like a gerbil. Or maybe a hamster, but not a rat. Constance couldn't take him seriously, and remained silent.

"In my day," he continued, "there was only one slut in each grade, with maybe another added senior year. You know, the one who got mono and didn't graduate."

Slut. Such an ugly word, nothing soft in its sibilance, so roughly snapped off with the hard tee at the end. Constance stared at the mobile line of his mouth, thin and unpromising.

"But it wouldn't be surprising to find out I really didn't know what was going on. I mean, I'm remembering this more or less from the outside. Appearances might not be everything. What do you think? How many girls were sluts in your school?"

"It was a *very* exclusive girls' school," Constance said. Then, less coldly, she added, "All of them."

"Constance, come in and meet our new neighbour," Eleanor called. There was a man on the couch beside her. "Ted, this is my daughter. Constance, this is Mr. Crofts. Mr. Crofts has that delightful little shop on Newbury we passed by the other day, with the carved lions on the steps. He's come to help me sort through some of this clutter."

On the table in front of them was a group of silver cases, hand-blown decanters and paperweights, and the crystal-domed music box from Constance's vanity table. It had been hers since her sixth birthday. When the key at the bottom was turned and the box righted, a tiny ballerina raised herself *en pointe* and spun a delicate series of *fouettes* on cunningly articulated legs, ivory white with lipstick-red slippers.

"That's mine," Constance said, the words coming from her mouth without volition, an automatic declaration of ownership.

"Of course, dear." Her mother fixed her with a smile. "But it's a little girlish, don't you think? Not really something for a young woman to keep. And you should be thinking about how much room you're going to have in your own place." To Ted, as if to qualify what she'd said, she added, "Constance starts her last year at Parson's in the fall. After that, I'm afraid I'll lose her to college."

Eleanor turned back to Constance, eyebrows slightly arched, and in the look that passed between them Constance understood she couldn't afford to claim anything as her own; her grades were such that she would never receive a scholarship, not to a good school. Everything had its price. Her only currency was acquiesence.

"I was just surprised to see it," she said. "I haven't thought about it in years."

Ted had the music box in his hands. His belt buckle glowed through the dome, distorted by the crystal, lighting an arc golden as a sunrise. The dancer's legs trembled, then slid to one side, an oblique line from her waist to the clear wall around her.

"A pretty thing," he said. His thumb stroked the crystal. "I'm not at all sure it's valuable in and of itself, however. Still, as you say, for a young girl, yes."

He set it back on the table. One note played from the mechanism. Constance couldn't remember when it was last wound.

Ted Crofts lived a block away; the back of his house was visible from the Brinkholder's through a gap between the leafy tops of city trees. Eleanor speculated on a bachelor's need for such a large place.

"When the Jensens had it, she was always complaining about the size of the bedrooms. Too small, she said. But the ground floor has that huge morning room. And a formal dining room that can seat twenty, at least."

Constance pulled the cat onto her lap, trying to distract herself. Her mother was sounding like someone from a small town, gossiping about the neighbours. It was embarrassing. At least in a small town, she thought, they'd *know* who their neighbours were. Constance paused while stroking Agatha. But they *did* know their neighbours; even here, they found out. Every place must be the same. No matter where she moved, it would be a small town, or composed of small-town populations, several instead of one. Agatha butted against her chin. Constance reached up and pushed the flattened fur around the cat's head forward into a ruff.

"Fluff out your face," she whispered. "You don't want anyone to call you snakehead."

"He must do a lot of entertaining," Eleanor decided.

"Could be." Alex put the newspaper aside. "Crofts has more going for him than that shop. Not that it's not lucrative enough, with his prices. He's not taking anything on consignment, is he?"

"Not from us." Eleanor's voice was firm. "The estate pieces are only part of what he has though. His clientele seem to be people who want to buy the kind of things that have been in the family for years. Or look like they have. You could literally furnish a house all at once, if you didn't mind sharing someone else's taste. Constance, you were there, did you ever think so many people would want suede cushions?"

"It's a racial memory, Mom. In the old country their ancestors slept with the livestock."

In the weeks before Christmas Constance wrote her exams and did about as well as she'd expected. Although she'd promised herself she'd make more of an effort than she had in previous years—and *did* try harder—her English Lit. exam started to shimmer in front of her eyes. She had a quickening sensation of displacement, a feeling that the point of being tested was to survive the experience, to get the exam out of the way rather than to display what she'd learned during the year.

She read the question: *Why does Madame Bovary die?* The answer flowed out of her pen: *Because of the money.*

Although the classroom discussion had been filled with defences of passion and the horrors of boredom—what Constance and her peers that year called "bushwah morality"—she didn't add anything else and was pleased when the teacher seemed to accept responsibility for her brevity, if not to understand that any explanation would be superfluous. Merely gossip.

The teacher wrote, in the margin of the paper: *OK. I should have asked for more. C+*

A friend gave her a ride into Boston on the Tuesday before Thanksgiving, letting her off at the Symphony stop on Huntington so she'd be underground while she passed by her parents' place. They didn't expect her home until Wednesday afternoon. The large tote she carried contained one real change of clothes, sundries, and a small pile of stuff she needed laundered. She was spending the night with Owen in a hotel. They'd worked this out during the past Labor Day weekend, before she went back to Mass. Amherst. She hadn't seriously investigated transferring to be closer to him. B.U. was just too weird for consideration.

At Park St. she switched to the Red Line and rode the train to Harvard Square. Owen was in front of the Coop, where they'd arranged to meet, and they walked over to Pizzeria Regina.

There were a few girls there that Constance knew, but she and Owen joined a group of his friends at the big table against the narrow end of the room. She wouldn't sit with other women when she was with him; either it was all girls, or she was the single girl in a group of boys. If anyone invited a girl to join them, Constance would let Owen know it was time for him to suggest they get moving on. She never examined that, she didn't even notice it happened, but other girls did. Guys wouldn't notice. Those kinds of details were like housework to them; rub their noses in it and all they do is look confused.

Once she was married she allowed herself to have women friends. The group might have appeared from the outside to be a professional network, as this is what such things were called. During a long evening of chocolate desserts at a South End condo, they started telling stories about their parents (mostly now in their seventies and needing assistance, if not support), although these seemed to end up as stories about being their parents' children.

Christine was the least-known to Constance, being a working mother. She was with a company developing the Harbour, picking up properties at three dollars a square foot and not doing much more than bring them up to code before they were flipped at one-hundred plus.

"It was just weird, once I was safely married and pregnant, it was like my mother entered some kind of time-warp. In her mind it was Baby-Chrissie-is-going-to-be-a-Mommy, as if none of that screaming at me in my teens had ever happened, calling me a tramp and threatening me with reform school.

"And it's not like Preston didn't know I had a past. It was just one of those things we didn't talk about. Still don't. And quite rightly. I don't want to know who he was screwing before me.

"Anyway, there we are at Thanksgiving dinner. I'm seven months and counting, and my mother is going on about how she can't believe her little girl is going to have a baby. Pres is giving me these looks across the table, sort of, Enough, already. It *was* getting a little sugary.

"And then she comes out with, 'It seems like only yesterday she was propping open the basement window so her little boyfriends from the football team could sneak in and visit at night.'"

Constance laughed as much as anyone else, although she was a little uncomfortable hearing a woman say "screwing." Before she could stop herself, she was telling about meeting Owen for—she searched for an airy, distancing phrase—a clandestine encounter.

"Clandestine encounter?" one of the women hooted. "Don't tell me *kisses* were exchanged."

"Something like that." Constance pressed her fork into some cake crumbs, but didn't raise it to her mouth. "He didn't get it, either. We were supposed to go someplace, not a ratty dump but, you know, anonymous. Instead, and I guess he thought this would be romantic, he booked a room at the Copley.

"So we, uh, exchanged kisses and, during the night, I got my period."

"Great timing," one of the women laughed, as another shrieked, "Julia!"

"What?"

"That's what my mother always called it: A visit from Julia."

"Julia and the Jets," Christine sputtered, a moment later asking, "Aren't the Jets a football team?"

"I had to go out first thing, of course," Constance said. "I took the elevator to the lobby, the doors opened, and my father was *right there.* I almost died."

"My god, what did he say?"

"Nothing. I let the doors close in front of me and went back to the room. We never mentioned it."

"What was *he* doing there?" someone asked.

"I don't know." Constance didn't consider that, didn't elaborate. Her father had died nine years earlier, nearly twenty years after that Thanksgiving. She couldn't be disloyal. She looked down at her cake, at the pinky-brown bubbles rising, and swallowed. "I felt like he'd seen me in my nightgown," she whispered.

Alex had held out as long as he could, going so far as to draw a demand note from a savings and loans after his own bank—where his father had banked before him—refused to advance him any more money. Finally, when even his physical posture suggested a man with his back to the wall, he sold his tar-sands options.

"It's no where near what they're worth," he said. "But we'll get by. Damn. They're going to be worth a million."

"Oh, a *million.*" Eleanor waved away the munificence of such a sum. She started into the kitchen, then turned back. "I'm just going to check on what we have for dinner. Maybe you could make me a cocktail?"

"Let me give you a hand," Constance said.

"That's all right. You can keep your father company."

"Really," Constance insisted. "It's about time I learned my way around a kitchen."

"From *me?* You know I never took things like that seriously. If anything, I'm sure you could teach me a thing or two. I don't know what you could be thinking."

"Then how about, I need the practice?"

She had earned her degree and was working at a public relations office in Rochester, renting a tiny apartment for a year to qualify for state-resident tuition at SUNY Binghamton. Her parents had given her Eleanor's Polaroid stock, as a graduation present. If she was careful, she could earn her independence through a doctorate. She'd been slightly taken aback by how little her grades mattered for her acceptance. It seemed that a few calls from her advisor was all that was required.

When Owen said he knew someone who could help her find a place to live, she agreed. They were seeing other people by then, although they'd never had a quarrel, never broken up. Owen was committed to business school. She was doing what she had to do. There was no way for them to be a couple. The logistics were impossible.

On East Avenue, in the high hundreds, the building was about twenty years old, built during an era of slap-dash construction, and lacking grace. But the apartment was self-contained, and Constance thought she'd prefer that to living in a renovated house, where she might have to walk through someone else's quarters to reach her own. And, in fact, living in the ugliest building on the block meant her view was of more attractive residences. A year didn't seem such a long time, after all.

Mr. Archer, the superintendent, was more than helpful while Owen and she moved in the things she had taken front her parents' house. None of the furniture was from her own room at home. Oddly, no matter what she took, including the mahogany suite from the third-floor guest room, her parents' house never seemed changed, never emptier or hollow with loss. Superficial skin wounds, was what she thought, able to heal without scarring.

Archer—Constance had automatically dropped the *Mr.*—gave instructions for loading the elevator most efficiently, even humped the mattresses from the U-Haul and put them up against the wall. He had a key to keep the elevator in service and insisted on riding up with Constance each trip, leaving Owen on the street to keep an eye on the van. His T-shirt was greyed and shrunken, ending inches above the belt of his low-slung green trousers. No matter where Constance looked, it seemed the widening line of rust hairs below his navel was in her peripheral vision; they or the darker, damp curls under the shirt's pushed-back sleeves. She stared at the floor numbers above the door and wasn't really listening when he asked if Owen was her boyfriend. She carelessly answered, "No."

"Oh, your brother?"

And, again, she made a mistake, although not the one she thought, answering, "I'm an only child."

Owen didn't stay over, although she issued an invitation which sounded, even to her, strangely formal. On the sidewalk, she almost put out her hand for him to shake, but he bent quickly and kissed her, missing her cheek and touching his lips to her neck.

In the morning, she had a moment's confusion on waking, thinking he had come back, hearing him in the other room.

"Owen?" She belted her robe as she walked down the short hall. Only the shortness of breath at her shock, seeing Archer in the middle of her living room, kept her from screaming.

"Morning," he said, too cheerfully. "I thought you might be able to use some of these things." He indicated the three green plastic bags at his feet, a ratty willow basket chair with an elasticized floral cover that looked chewed and mauled.

"Okay," Constance said, taking a step back and tipping her head towards the bedroom. "I'll ask my friend what he wants to do with it."

His face tensed. There was a long pause before he said, "Yeah, right. Well, whatever you decide you want."

"Thank you." Her voice was level. "Please don't trouble yourself any more. I really won't need your help for the rest of the things that need to be done. I've already made arrangement for replacing the washer in the shower, checking that fuse on the stove...replacing the locks."

After he was gone, unable to quite leave with the cocky assurance he was so clearly aiming for, Constance opened one of the plastic bags, using only the very tips of her fingers. There was a Teflon frying pan of lightweight aluminum, obviously cheap even when new and now scratched beyond all practical use, a bent and chipped set of tin canisters, a steel colander with crusty orange rings around the holes.

This was beyond junk, it was *garbage.* The word came to her with a rush of images. At the Porter school, in her home room, she had been responsible for the gerbil cage. On Mondays, before class, she replaced the old litter with fresh curls of planed, sweet, cedar. She kept the gerbil in an empty chalk box while she did, and then, after she returned it to its cleaned cage, she would put in a cardboard centre from a roll of toilet paper. The little rodent would appear ecstatic, eyes closed while it shredded the tube into a fluffy nesting material. Constance had thought it was in gerbil-heaven, delirious with purposeful activity, making its own bed.

What if it was, instead, feeling like *this?* The idea—that

she had tormented a helpless animal, however inadvertently—was too poignant to consider.

She examined what had been dumped on her, pushing her fists into her throat, blocking the sound she felt there, when she looked into the bottom of one bag. Keeping the plastic between the object and her naked toes, she poked and prodded until it was on the floor. She laughed, then, having uncovered not, as she'd feared, an enema bag, but a little girl's plastic handbag with a long shoulder strap. A pink starfish was glued to its side.

The rest of the day passed harmlessly, a series of benign accomplishments, and Constance slid between her sheets with a delicious satisfaction.

At first she was watching herself from a great distance, in the manner of dreams, as she danced in Copely Square. She seemed to be wearing a body stocking covered with hundreds of fine diamonds; her every movement set her sparkling, created an aura of pure light. Under her feet, the ground was dull as base metal. From her superior vantage she could see people exiting the stores along Stuart and Boylston. They lined the sidewalks. Some stepped down into the street, although none crossed the white line. Without actually identifying the real place, she was aware of the rooftop of her own house, aware of the lives under that tarry surface. A moment later, as she executed a willowy pirouette, she became aware that people on the park benches were getting up and moving away from her, joining the others in the street. A dense wall of humanity was forming around, away, from her dance. In an instant, she was back in her body, seeing through her own eyes. Her arm, a delicate arc in front of her body, glistened. She admired her hand, the flashing points of light beginning at her wrist, moving up her arm. Droplets of water, she thought, until her focus narrowed on the motion. Not flowing: crawling up her arm. On articulated legs of polished metal, eight to each crystal centre. Her naked skin was covered with tiny, mechanical spiders, thousands of them. She turned clumsily, in a jerky, staggered, circle, holding her arms away from her body. The faces around her blurred into an anonymous band of white, pink, tan indifference. Nobody moved towards her.

She wanted to call out, to cry for help, but she had to keep her lips pressed tightly together, muted by fear, horrified that one of the animated creations might enter her mouth.

Recession. Stagflation. Hyper-inflation. The economists had names for it, even if they couldn't agree among themselves about what was happening. For Constance, it meant that her teaching assistant's stipend was a dollar number that sounded like a year's wages, although it lasted only a couple of months. One time, feeling admirably resourceful, she wore to class a kilt she'd owned since she was sixteen. It fit fine, but she spent the day under the eyes of men who seemed to think that she was in costume for their titillation.

She chipped away at what was left of the Polaroid stock, having halved the amount with her purchase of a '71 Gremlin. The savings from good gas milage should have made up for the nickel and dime repairs that were necessary, but oil had shot past seventeen dollars a barrel and people were treating a tank of gas with the reverence once reserved for home ownership.

She had to postpone leaving for Boston until an odd-numbered day, when she could join a block-long line-up at the gas station. Things were tough all over, but the only change in Back Bay, evidently, was that Ted Crofts had a new woman in his life.

"Absolutely useless, of course. You know the type," Eleanor told her. "Divorced."

"There's a lot of it going around," Constance said, turning away from the Christmas tree. She thought it was the smallest they'd ever had; the decorations seemed to be weighing it down. The metallic red and green balls looked vulgar on the ends of its branches. There was a box by her side, of glass angels from Germany that she hadn't yet taken out of the tissue paper.

"I haven't heard of any divorces around here. Who on earth could you be thinking of?"

"Well, other people." Constance shrugged. Stepping back, she squinted to blur her focus, then started removing the balls. Everything in icy silver, she decided. A winter tree. "You know, *them.*"

"Her name's Ruthie." Eleanor leaned forward, putting her book on the couch beside her. "I saw her when I was coming out of the library. I guess she was going to Lord and Taylor, away from the Square, at any rate. Anyway, what I wanted to tell you," she lowered her voice, confidingly. "She was in this two-piece outfit, like pyjamas, almost.

Stretchy nylon knit with," she fixed Constance with a look, "a leopard print."

"Really?" Constance shook her head, properly appalled. She felt relaxed for the first time since she'd come home for the holiday. She felt like a daughter, and took a place on the couch, pulling her feet up under her. "What time was it?"

"Well, after *two,*" Eleanor conceded. "But before five."

They basked in a companionable silence for a moment, like two seals on a smooth rock. Then Constance asked, "I wonder if they let her in?"

"Who, dear?"

"Lord and Taylor."

Together, they raised their hands and made clawing motions in the air. In unison they said, "Meow, meow," and laughed softly.

"So, of course," Eleanor said, as though completing a thought. "I volunteered your services when he asked for help with his party. Especially when he made it clear you were invited on your own, not just with us. *She* won't be able to do anything."

"Mom, jeez." Constance got up and went back to the tree, charged now with being more than the daughter she wanted to be. She was twenty-six years old and almost a Ph.D.. "What am I going to have to do?"

"He wants you to show him how to make bread. I think you should welcome the opportunity to get to know him better. He knows a lot of people, people you might want to be introduced to when you graduate. Oh, the German angels! Let me help you."

As Constance stretched up to hang a silvery snowflake, it caught the light and reflected her own face, with her mother's profile behind it. Time seemed to ripple in an elastic loop around Constance; she had a sense of generations of women, as strong a presence in the room, as the scent of balsam, all engaged in the small ceremonies of life, the rituals of continuance. She thought her heart might break.

"You don't have to go over to Ted's," her mother said. "I can call and tell him you're busy, if you like."

"No, that's okay. I'll do it." Constance tapped a hanging angel, set it on a lazy twirl. Light flashed like swordplay over its flawless surface, shards of all colours or no colour.

Eleanor passed her another angel, saying, "I can imagine, when he sees these, he'd kill to get them for the shop. But they're staying in the family. I want to see them on your daughter's tree."

Constance looked at the angel in her hand, felt it poreless and perfect against her skin. Eleanor had been thirty-seven when Constance was born. Her back was starting to develop a hump. Some of her dresses fit on her as though they'd been fashioned with deep darts and she was wearing them backwards. That spring, she'd fallen in the bathroom, and her shoulder had taken months to heal. She seemed to be inches shorter, and there was a slight, but real, tremor in her hands. Constance turned away to hang the angel.

I'm putting jewellery on a dead tree, she thought. *What a pagan thing to do.*

Ruthie may not have been useless, but her competence was never put to the test. She sat on a stepladder in one corner of the kitchen, never lifting a finger, while Constance washed bowls and measuring cups during the dough's proofing.

"It's sort of understood as the first line in every recipe," she told the older woman pointedly, passing a pyrex cup to Ted, who was drying. "'Fill the sink with hot, soapy water.' That way, when you're done, you're done."

"I'll have to remember to tell that to the girl who does that for me," Ruthie said. "Not that I ever have her make bread. No carbohydrates, or I'll look like my sister. It's not a tough choice."

"Like, living here or being out on the street?" Ted asked. "Five pounds, tops, and you're out of here."

Constance bent down and reached into the open oven, where the bread was rising with the heat of the pilot light. She lifted the dish towel and poked a dimple into the dough, watched it fill in, smooth as a baby's cheek.

"This is ready to be turned out," she said, wiping the sleeve of her sweater across her hot forehead. Under her hands, the dough was warm and elastic, slightly resistant to her touch.

"Sort of *persuade* it," she told Ted. "Gently." But he couldn't master the technique. His fingertips raked through the dough; his thumbs gouged and tore. She stopped herself from looking in Ruthie's direction and flushed with an unavoidable thought: *Is this how he touches your breasts?*

The image of his hands stayed with her, shamefully, for

the rest of the day. At the party, with his house full of people, she kept herself moving, passing trays of rumaki and raw vegetables, carrying abandoned glasses into the kitchen. She was running water into a sherry schooner someone had used as an ashtray when Ted came up behind her, reaching over to turn off the tap.

"You don't have to do that," he said, taking her damp hand in his. "Come on, there's something I want you to see."

He pulled her up the back stairs to the third floor. It was easier for her to follow him than to find her own way, up or down, on her own. The hall was dark but he didn't hesitate, tapping a wall switch as he drew her into a room at the top of the house.

"My study," he said, nudging her forward. He stepped back and remained in the doorway, using the insides of his wrists to tug up his trousers.

Constance stood in the middle of the small, dormered room, lit only to a pink dimness by a heavily-shaded bulb. Across from the windows was a sleek desk, like an architect's drawing table. Beside it was a grey metal filing cabinet. This starkness was in contrast to an overstuffed arm chair and square end table with an elaborately carved pedestal, in the window's recess. On the tabletop was a cut-glass ashtray, a pair of binoculars, a small box of tissues, and a crystal-domed music box.

Constance took a step forward, turned, turned back, and lifted the familiar object. The dancer trembled. She forced her eyes away, looked quizzically at Ted.

"This was sold," she said.

"I bought it, for the shop," he agreed. "But then I couldn't bring myself to part with it. Why don't you try the field-glasses?"

"Yes?"

She put the music box back on the table, reluctantly, and picked up the binoculars. The barrels were coated with a thick, grey rubber, an overly-masculine material unpleasant to her touch. Where she was standing it was automatic that, as she raised the glasses to her eyes, she was aiming her enhanced vision through the window. The focus was acute; she could see clearly.

She was looking into her own bedroom. Her room as a child, as a teenager; the room she'd slept in all this week. On the foot of her bed, visible in the pool of light from her bedside lamp, Agatha was lying, her back legs stretched out and demurely crossed at the ankles, like an actress/model on the hood of a car at the auto show. The glasses were powerful enough for Constance to see a flick of the cat's pink tongue against the greying snout as she licked the edge of a front paw, prepatory to washing her face.

With the glasses still up to her face, she closed her eyes. She was aware that Ted had come farther into the room, was almost behind her. In a move that was unplanned, and perhaps graceful as a result, she put the binoculars back on the table and picked up the music box.

"I guess I'll take this back." she said. "I don't think you really paid enough for it, not what it's worth."

Whatever he responded, she didn't know. She never knew how she made it down the dark stairs and out of the house. All she knew was that sometime later she was back in her parents' living room with the dancer twirling under her crystal dome. One of the teeth of the music mechanism must have become fatigued and broken off. There was a moment's silence in the middle of the tune, a moment that held the last note's remembrance.

She didn't hear her parents come home. They might have been tired and gone right to bed, or they might have seen her on the couch and decided to let her sleep, maybe having a drink in the kitchen and discussing the party in lowered voices. When she woke up it was dark and someone had spread an afghan over her, or she'd pulled it down from the camel-back chair. She lifted her head, foul-mouthed and disoriented. Her legs were too heavy to swing to the floor. She reached behind her, under her sweater, and unhooked her bra, slid its straps down her arms and over her hands, wadded it under the cushions beneath her head. She was almost asleep again when Agatha jumped up onto the couch and started treading on her stomach, kneading her flesh.

"Stop that," she whispered, pushing the aged animal away. "Get down. I'm not your mother."

Owen's engagement and marriage had been announced in the paper. Constance didn't recognize the bride's name and, of course, there wasn't a photograph, but she imagined her to be one of those tense women, prone to spells and nervous when too far from their beds. Owen was listed as being with a major brokerage house, but the phrasing was ambiguous, and he wasn't given a title. She told herself she didn't much care, was much too busy that year, sending out applications for positions that would take her away from the one she had. It wasn't even tenure track and she didn't know how her mother was going to take it when she finally had to confess that it was not only a junior college, but a Catholic one. Most likely her mother already knew—these institutions were not exactly *secret*—but she would wait to hear the confession from Constance herself, not bring it up on her own.

When Eleanor called, to tell her that Alex had been taken to the hospital, Constance asked, "What for?" Casually, she asked the question, as if the answer might have been some uncomplicated, elective surgery: the removal of a mole, hair transplants.

She put down the phone and looked around the apartment the college had provided. Nothing here was anything she needed, nothing she would want to take with her. She picked up the phone again, called the department secretary and asked her to cancel her class. No, she didn't know for how long. Yes, she knew the sessional lecturer would be paid out of her salary, if one had to be hired. The mid-term grade reports were coming due. Two copies, orange for the department, blue for the registrar. And next week was a Holy Day of Obligation. Yes, yes, thank you, damn you.

And then she was on the road, averting her eyes each time she passed a rest area with a pay phone. She forced herself to not keep glancing at her watch. Time didn't matter. Her father would hold on until she was there, if he wanted to, if he thought it was necessary. The decision was his to make, to decide if saying goodbye was important. People could do that. They did it all the time, then their families wrote heart-warming stories and sent them to *Reader's Digest.* Her mind skittered away from the phrase "unforgettable character." It sounded like "remembered as something other than human."

Agatha had been put down in the spring, when her hips made the stairs impossible.

Constance didn't stop at the house first, but drove straight to the hospital. Her skin was crawling with tension. The car was slowing her down; she could have run the last miles in less time. She thought that, at one time, this level of energy was normal to her, yet she hadn't noticed any seeping out, any slipping away.

At the Admissions desk, a nurse or receptionist directed her to Information, a long hall away.

"That's where they keep that, uh, information," she said. "So if you'll follow the blue line painted on the floor, Mrs.—"

"He was admitted *here,"* Constance said sharply. "So you must have some record of where he was taken. And it's not *Mrs.,* it's *Doctor* Brinkholder."

Astonishing, the difference that made. On the sixth floor, a black nurse who looked about eighteen led her directly to a waiting room. Before she could ask about her mother, her father's cardiologist was standing beside her, flipping back sheets of paper held in a metal clipboard, and explaining his diagnosis, his procedures.

He was less than a head taller than she was in flats. By lifting up on her toes, she could nibble his ear. He smelled of hard soap and spearmint, with a hint of a more natural odour. She could put her arm around his waist, under the back of his white coat, slide it down to his belt, inside his chalk-stripe trousers. She could tug his pants to his ankles and throw him down on the floor. She could ride him like Malabar.

Alex died under heavy sedation, without speaking.

Constance suggested a smaller place, either an apartment or condo. Travel? Some sort of classes? She couldn't think of any other diversions, and started again on the size of the house, its unnecessary burden.

"I don't know what you mean." Eleanor looked around vaguely. They were in the kitchen nook, the room with fewest associations, although neither of them had consciously made that point. Constance had slept on the living room couch, claiming she was too tired to carry her suitcase up the stairs.

"This is a white elephant," Constance repeated. "Everyone is scaling down."

"Oh, yes. Yes. You know, at one time I thought you'd raise your family here. We'd move to Arizona or something, and stay on the top floor, here, for holidays. Can you imagine? And now you're telling me to sell."

"You'll need the income," Constance pointed out.

"Um." Eleanor got up and stood in front of the sink. "Well, that's out of the question, isn't it?"

"You're going to have to make a decision of some kind." Constance looked away as her mother reached behind the curtain for her gin-and-tonic on the windowsill. "Soon."

"Why are you so determined to get me out of here? I've told you, I *can't* sell the house. It's already sold."

"Sold! No," Constance shook her head. She wondered if her mother was suffering stress trauma, or in a fugue state, escaping into some other world, one with softer edges, fewer choices. The doctor might have given her something. "How could it be sold?"

"One way or another." Eleanor shrugged, indifferent. She crossed the room and took down the bottle of gin, openly this time. "Something came up. I'm not sure I quite remember what it was, that time. Just one more thing, I guess. Anyway, I have a few years left on the lease-back. We'll talk then."

Constance got up and reached for a glass of her own. She watched her hand on the cupboard door. It looked as it always had, only now the door was a stranger's. The hand was the hand of a guest in a tenant's residence.

"Arizona," her mother said, very quietly. "But not Phoenix."

"Irish," Eleanor sniffed, dismissing the idea of a viewing. Instead, the funeral home provided a fairly large room with a lectern for the memorial record, a dozen chairs against two walls. There was a low, round table in the centre of the room, with a floral arrangement that looked more festive than funereal. White mums.

Constance waved away cigar smoke exhaled by an elderly man. She had no idea who he was and didn't risk a cutting remark, but she kept him in a corner of her vision, to see what he was going to do with his ashes. *I'm worrying about* ashes *in a funeral home.* She caught herself before laughing, and nodded a welcome to a couple who were standing in the doorway. The woman was wearing cocktail-length black jersey and Constance was suddenly furious. Her brow creased and she scanned the room for her mother, to share a raised eyebrow at such inappropriateness.

"Owen!" She hadn't seen him arrive. "I really didn't expect to see you here," she said, to explain her surprise.

"You didn't?" He looked confused or hurt. "You thought I wouldn't hear about this? You thought I wouldn't come? Wait, sorry, I'm not here to drill you with questions. What I mean to say is, I'm sorry about your loss. I am. Truly."

"Yes," she said. "Okay, yes. And *you,* as well; I understand congratulations are in order. So, congratulations. And you're well and happy? You look good."

"Do I?" He sounded pleased. He looked at the backs of his hands. "Marriage agrees with me?"

"I guess it must do," she said. "And is she here?" The name escaped her.

"No, unfortunately she couldn't make it."

He started to make his apology for her absence but, over his shoulder, Constance saw Ted and Ruthie come into the room, and she stepped closer to him, and said in a low voice, "Get me out of here. Please, get me someplace else."

Legal Seafoods was too crowded for them to get a table. They sat at one of the bars in the centre of the room, shared with a trio of women who were brightly made-up and dressed, perhaps, for a summer evening in a tropical climate. Dressed to work the streets of the Combat Zone. Even in the soft light, they looked toughened and slightly pathetic.

Constance ordered for the two of them, crab cakes and mugs of beer.

"Like the old days," she said, when the food was in front of them, her first beer replaced.

"Is it?" Owen put his fork down and straightened his tie. "Yes, I suppose it is. Of course it is. Doesn't that seem like it was a lifetime ago?"

"Not to me," Constance protested. She was making an effort to keep her head level. "To me, it's like last week, only very far off to one side, like I could find my way back there, if I only knew how. And then I could start going forward, without ending up here."

"I don't think—" Owen started, but they were both diverted by the trio of women, rising in a group and leaving, a musky cloud hanging in the air after them. One made a comment about having to change her clothes, that she'd never be able to strip out of what she was wearing.

"If I bent over to get these over my feet," she said, "they'd be looking right up to my kidneys."

"That place," Owen shook his head.

"You don't see that every day," Constance said. "A snatch of exotic dancers." She made a disgusting noise, like a wet snigger, and flagged a hand at a waiter, pointing to her mug of beer, drained, with a lacy lining of foam.

"Are you sure you really want another?" Owen asked.

"It can't hurt. This is one of those nights I couldn't get

drunk if I tried." She turned to the waiter, who seemed to be trying to slip past her, looking into the air over her head. "Hey, you, could I get some *service* here?"

When her senses returned, she was in the back of Owen's BMW. At first she thought the enveloping odour was vomit, before she recognized the redolence of leather. Her dress was pushed up under her breasts, a ropy girdle. She could feel the shreds of her pantyhose tickling over one thigh, and feel her unshod feet in the night air. Owen was already inside her and pumping like a derrick.

"Oh god," she moaned. Her mouth tasted of blood.

"Catch up," he gasped. "I started without you."

She arced up against him, straining and urgent, and found the rhythm, a rhythm that filled her mind, beating: *marry me marry me marry*

The subpoena arrived on the same day as the invitation to the gala. The Museum of Fine Art had made a purchase of Leonardo da Vinci drawings, hitherto presumed lost. Owen was implicated in an insider-trader suit.

"I don't want to be out there looking like one of those guys on the news with his jacket over his head," he said. "Or smiling and acting like nothing is wrong." He was sitting on the edge of the bed, although Constance has told him, and more than once, that he'll ruin the mattress. He was wearing white boxer shorts of Sea Island cotton and his pubic hair was a dark shadow through the fabric; his penis was outlined against the top of his right leg, shrunken. They hadn't made love, not since the lawyers said the brokers weren't responsible for legal fees. Not that Owen needed a defence attorney, only counsel.

"You're a *witness,"* Constance snapped. "You were only a consultant. It's not like you profited from what everyone, and I mean everyone, was doing."

"It's the same brush," he ran a hand through his hair, then looked at his fingers, checking for fall-out. "And where do you think our money came from? I was making a good living."

"A good living?" Constance turned to him from the vanity mirror, then turned back to watch him in mirror-image. "A good living," she repeated, "what's *that?"* She began to trace the line of her upper lip with a small brush. Thirty-six hundred a month for the home they'd found for her mother. Anything less and there'd be drooling idiots. She started on her lower lip. Thank god she'd never smoked, or needed electrolysis; she was spared those spidery lines running up to her nose.

"Some people might think it was enough."

"We're not some people. Christine says there's a very good chance she can get me on the board, and I'm not having it ruined by you acting like you're guilty. We'll get through this. We will." She dropped a silk scarf over her head, then slid her arms into her dress, raised it above her shoulders, and let it drop down. The stitching behind the beading was a little scratchy, even through her slip. Cheap labour, she thought, Korean. And they used to use silk thread, not this stuff that felt like fishing line.

"Now get into your tux and I'll do your tie for you."

Constance moved away from the man who looked like a gerbil. His name was Jeff, and he was Canadian, which she thought explained a lot. She noticed he never let a waiter pass by without taking another glass of champagne. The kind of man who approaches a lady not of his acquaintance and says *slut.*

She looked at the drawings, arranged behind thick acrylic panels. Protective. The drawings of men were like anatomical illustrations, or photographs, with every detail sharply delineated. But the women, spread out as though flung down against a hard surface, were precisely exact except for the space between their legs, which was only a smudged blur of charcoal, a hasty slash made while looking away. Jeff was behind her, following, and she tried to muster some charity. He was so out of place. Then his hand was on her arm, pressing, and she was about to slap his face when his voice barked out in a hoarse whisper, "Oh my God. Would you look over there? I mean, I've heard about visible panty-line, but who'd wear white wool over an *adult diaper?"*

Unable to help herself, she glanced in the direction indicated by his eyes. She almost laughed out loud. It was Ruthie, and she did have some odd sort of bunching at the back of her dress.

"Actually, I know her," she said.

"Oh, *no,"* he said. "I was just, you know, surprised to see such a stereotype. Isn't that just *exactly* the picture of the American divorcee?"

"She *is* divorced," Constance said, meaning; once

divorced, always a divorcee. "Shall I introduce you?"

"Oh, honey," he said. "What would I do with a woman like that? I'm queer as a *tree.*"

"How interesting," Constance said and, not without irony, thought how pleased her mother would be with her manners. She asked, as though inquiring about his job, "And how long have you been, uh, gay?"

"Since I was fourteen," he said, hardly raising his hand to stop a passing waiter for another class of champagne. They seem to know each other, the two of them, some message passes between their eyes. "The year before, Diane Waldo used to lure me into her garage and read me the dirty bits from her mother's books, but that year I got my hands on my very own copy of *Peyton Place.* Paperback, with those creases in the spine.

"I read that thing with eyes like a *panda,* and on, I think page 264, Betty had Rodney in the car and was doing—well, I don't know what she was doing—but she asked, 'Is it up? Is it up good and hard?' And Rodney, uh, sort of allowed as to how it was. And she, Betty, said, 'Good. Go stick it in Alison MacKenzie.'

"My ears got so hot that I could smell singed hair. I looked up at the wall across from me, and I thought, 'I guess I'd better sleep with *men.*'

"Jesus," Jeff looked at the ceiling, "really I'm not like this at all."

"Don't worry, I'm not shocked," Constance said. "I'm the one who got you started, and it's a cute story."

"A cute story?" Jeff's breath was hot with wine. "How

could you think that was *cute?* And it's certainly not a *story.*"

Constance looked at his eyes, glassy and possibly crazed, and thought about turning her head to one side and calling, "Security!" But, at that moment, Ruthie floated over.

"Connie! I didn't expect to see you here, not tonight." She put one arm up to Constance's shoulder, although she didn't allow any weight to press against her. "I'm so sorry about this little nastiness I've been following in the paper. You must be worried sick. And this awful war. I don't believe for a minute it's not about oil."

"We're going to be fine," Constance said, noting that Jeff was looking back and forth between her and Ruth. She tried to imagine what he was thinking, if he thought she and Ruthie were contemporaries. The difference in their ages wasn't all that great, she realized with some surprise. And Ruthie's face-lift had left her skin smooth, unlined, although there was a dead-looking patch at the tip of her nose.

At the front of the room, a lanky man, at least in his sixties, approached the podium. She looked around for Owen, but couldn't pick him out of any group of tuxedoed men. Turning to Ruthie, she said, "Is Ted here?"

The man at the front of the room started speaking into a microphone, his voice electronic and removed from the conversation.

"Ted?" Ruthie repeated. Then, again, "Ted?" She looked at Jeff, narrowing her eyes as though he were keeping some secret from her.

"Ted Crofts," Constance said. "Ted."

"Why would he be here?"

"I'm sorry, I thought you two were married. I'm sure I heard that somewhere."

"Married? God, no. You don't have to put a ring through the bull's nose when you've already got him by the horns."

At the front of the room, the man was introducing the curator of the exhibit, a man who seemed to have an intimate knowledge of the provenance of the Leonardo drawings.

"...disappeared in the seventeenth century," he said.

The drawings sat on their easels. Constance glanced at them, hardly registering their images. She looked over to where Jeff stood, with a finger raised to the centre of one drawing of a woman, a small smile on his face.

"...reportedly in Vichy France...."

"Why *bother?*" Her voice filled the open atrium. The echo of it returned to her, but the sound wasn't enough to stop her from speaking again. Her voice was febrile and arresting. "What's the point?" she demanded. "Why didn't someone just *burn* them?"

HEAVEN FULL OF ASTRONAUTS

Saturday is slipping by the car windows, another August afternoon, another distraction making its claim on his attention. Montreal may be a hundred miles to the east, Ottawa sixty miles north. Charles does not have a sharp sense of direction. His mind is wandering, although he's also trying to maintain some alertness to Carole's voice, in case she dips into an interrogative. He doesn't want to have to turn, blinking, to ask, "What?" He has enough unanswered questions of his own.

"I have to go back to this place, where I used to spend summers with my family," Carole said. "It's a personal thing, but I'd like it if you came with me. Unless you're doing something else that weekend?"

Charles did have the time before classes started again in the fall. He was certainly interested in spending the time with her; they seemed to be stuck at an arm's length after eight or ten months together. He asked, "Is this something serious? Is there anything I can do?"

But he wasn't sure what he was offering her, or what he could do. His response was a mannered one.

And she said, "You could just be there, and not ask any questions. I can't promise I'll be the best company, but I'd rather not be alone."

"Okay," Charles agreed. But he added, "Why me?"

"You always look a little confused when people use words like moon or stars, as if they were abstract concepts. This way, even if you have a lousy time, you could write it off as a learning experience. Although they always seem to teach you something else, don't they?"

"I do that, really?" Charles asked, taking no offense, flattered that he had received the attention, that he was noticed. He considered his apparent reaction to those simple nouns, moon and stars. How long would it take, he wondered, before everything ceased to be new?

Since reading a news magazine's cover story on the arms race, he's been haunted by a phrase that may describe the shortness of his own future. Of any future. The phrase is *enrichment facility.* This sounds like something wonderful but, like *exceptional child* or *artificial heart,* the reality needs the context of faith in human nature, or trust in social conditions, to have any meaning at all. The words existed, with independent meaning, before this use; no intrinsic change has occurred.

Still, does the artificial heart make the body a machine? Is it possible plutonium, enriched, is no longer inanimate? If electrical energy defines brain life, why not include radioactivity? Is there a moral distinction buried in the premise? Maybe he's reading too much into the phrase, giving too much credit to the language of technology, or the use of language by technical persons.

In Carole's bathroom, not very long ago, he had discovered a clinical-looking tube of something, with letterng squared and official-looking as a computer print-out announcing a revolutionary formula of protein polypeptides. He'd thought, minimum, that the molecular secrets of DNA had been unravelled, that the origin and mystery of life had been decoded. All things were possible, even this happening without his awareness.

The tube had contained a hair conditioner.

More and more, Charles suspects he's walking through the real world a few steps behind.

Carole has an appliance she wears in her mouth when she sleeps, to keep her teeth from grinding and ruining her bite. Her dentist, the salesman, told her to consider it a small investment. "A couple hundred beans," he'd said in offhand response to her inquiry. But then he collected the cash, as usual. It's another kind of aggression, the way men get so coy about the demands they make of women. The deal was simple enough: he had a product she wanted to buy. This *beans* business only trivialized her part of the transaction.

With a conscious effort, she relaxes her grip on the steering wheel—the tension in her wrists had reminded her of her clenched jaws—and she glances over to Charles.

She thinks, not the first time, Who is he? Meaning,

What? A friend once said, "Charles? Oh, he's safe." The two women shared a complicit look. Now she knows it's not that (and she regrets her part of the exchange). Carole has never found weakness in Charles, only generosity. If he has a hard centre, he keeps it well concealed. Otherwise, if such a thing is possible, Charles is exactly what he appears to be. Even now, in the car, his expression is a gift.

"Are you starting to feel illicit?"

"What?" Charles turns to her, blinking. "Oh, yes," he says. "Something like that."

"What the English call a dirty weekend." Carole stresses the correct pronunciation, *wee-kend,* and Charles laughs. She remembers that he is not here for her reasons, and rushes to extend this moment. Even overt manipulations, direct statements of want, make her feel depressed and rotten. Rotting.

"The large plants you see on either side," she says in a plummy, authoritative voice, "are called trees. In the area above ground, between the car and these trees, invisible to you, is fresh air. It is considered healthful, in that it leaves no sludgy deposits on your lungs."

"Yes," Charles indicates the scenery. "Reminds me of Riverend."

"What's Riverend?"

"It's where I grew up. Small town. Not too far from here, I guess."

"I didn't know that about you." Carole checks the mirror before turning to him. "You seem so urban." She means his studio apartment in centretown; his knowledge of dry cleaners that do alterations; his use of the only place that delivers morning coffee and bagels. These are his workings of 'home' that she envies.

"There's not really much to know. There were trees and fresh air, sure, but we didn't have to search for them. They were a condition, not an experience."

"They were for me. Some of my earliest memories are of the drive up here, and the difference when we arrived, like a coolness, almost." Her voice changes tone, when she says *memories,* from contemplative to brusque. *"There's* something I don't know about you. What's your earliest memory?"

"That's an easy one. There was a night when the entire neighbourhood covered their back lawns with white bed-sheets. One of the first space flights was in an orbit that would take it overhead and we were determined we'd be noticed. Everyone stood by their own houses, not to blot the sheets, and stared up at the dark sky, trying to catch a glimpse of the moving light. Some people may have waved, in that slow, ceremonious *bon voyage* way."

Charles straightens the shoulder strap of his seatbelt, leans his elbow on the rim of the car window, and is silent for a moment.

"It was so quiet. An entire community with a single purpose, looking up at heaven. I can't imagine such a thing ever happening again."

"Was it enough to make you visible?" Carole asks. "Did the astronauts say anything?"

"This was before manned flights. It was a radio satellite,"

Charles says. "There was nobody to see us. I don't think the satellite even had photographic capabilities." He laughs, and slaps hard on the dashboard. "My god, there was no earthly point to it. I've known that for years, and this is the first time I've heard myself say it. My earliest memory, part of a mass delusion. Small towns. The unexamined life." He settles down, grinning now, but edgily. "No wonder I was in a hurry to get away."

"When did you leave?"

"For college, really," Charles says. "But it had stopped feeling like home before that. Things had changed. Then there was no reason to go back."

"But you've changed as well." Carole's hands tighten on the wheel. "You could go back, set things right. Even start over. Look at all the people buying up property and putting down roots in those places. There must be something to that kind of life."

"No," Charles says. "It's not really the life. Their choice might make them happy. If it doesn't, they can make another. We all end up being someplace. It's the choosing that matters."

"Standing in the dark, staring up into empty space." Carole tries to feel a part of the group, their straining silence. The feeling is, of course, hope. And a little bit more; an unspoken promise of deliverance. "I think I would make that my choice, to live where I could share something like that. I like the story."

"It didn't used to have a punch line," he says.

Charles pulls his arm in from the window, not wanting the darker band of sun- and wind-burned skin around his elbow branding him not only urban, but a non-driver as well. For this trip to the country he has chosen a tussah silk shirt with short sleeves, jeans new enough to be almost navy, and a pair of boots the colour of stained porcelain around a bathtub drain. These boots were made in Brazil for exotically narrow feet and in an hour or so Charles will be nearly crippled, his outside toes crushed flat. If they reach the lodge before that time, however, he'll be able to step out of the car, over six feet tall with an almost military bearing. This does not present a difficult trade-off, he thinks, comfort for command. Illusion of command.

A lodge on a fifty-acre lake less than ten miles from a small town; that couldn't cost a hundred dollars a night, could it? Charles has very little money until the beginning of September, and no credit cards at all. He's assuming that rustic alone is not much of a commodity. The big bucks go for isolation or anonymity, surely, following the law of supply and demand. Everybody wants to go someplace where nobody has been. There are magazines with huge circulations as a result of this individual desire. Charles shares a library carrel with a guy named Tony, in International Media, who is obsessed with the advertisements in *Travel and Leisure.*

"They're like blueprints for the experience. I think I have a handle on them now. It's in the relationship of bathing suit to age." Tony spread out full-page clippings over the blonde wood surface of the desk, shuffling a single page to the top. "This is your basic couple. He's in his early thirties, she's about the same. Late twenties. Younger women are still favourable, although the margin seems to be decreasing."

Charles looked at the picture, knowing he wasn't expected to comment. The woman in the ad was leaning at a difficult angle against some kind of tree, its foliage running into the margin. A man was apparently kneeling in front of her, his back and neck twisted in such a way his eyes were focused directly at the top of her thighs, where the bottom of her bathing suit v-ed like an arrowhead.

"Now, he's in trunks, and her two-piece is very conservative. This is a family-oriented place. They're married, but so far childless. If he was in briefs and her suit was smaller, they'd be having an affair, maybe having just met at the place itself."

"I see," Charles said, seeing nothing. He pulled a second ad to the top of the pile. "And?"

"Very good. The man in briefs and the same-age woman in a revealing one-piece. This is the one- or two-child body. The woman is divorced, financially independent, and available for instant sex. If the man wore trunks in this one, it might be a place to take the kids to get to know his new girlfriend, away from the disapproval of the ex-wife. Or even the kids alone, the father being sold on the myth of quality time."

Charles was flipping through the rest of the ads, nodding agreement. He was stopped by a page unlike the rest: even the photography was muted, overcast with grey. An older couple, fiftyish, walked down a beach, not sandy but pebbled, with a jutting of rock like a headstone behind them. The woman, in blown chiffon, carried a pair of evening shoes. The man was wearing rolled-up white ducks. His shirt was completely unbuttoned. His chest hair was grey but—Charles brought the picture closer to his face—the hair darkened as it approached his belt. Snow on the chimney? The man looked calmly pleased and relaxed. Turned to him, the woman's expression seemed to be...grateful?... concerned? The expression was unreadable, perhaps because of its nakedness.

Charles looked away. It was the most romantic evocation he'd ever seen.

"That's an interesting one. The woman's wrap is over a two-piece, but she's almost his age and handsome rather than provocative. I think it's a second honeymoon. The exposed chest, a well-used heart? No grandchildren. Grandchildren places have the woman in tennis whites, or co-ordinates. Sportive, but not irresponsible."

"It's breaking my heart," Charles said. He decided the man was recovering from by-pass surgery. Chest hair covered the surgical scars, explaining the lack of pigmentation and trousers masked the donor site of arteries on the man's legs. His wife's expression was relief. Thank god they could afford this vacation. They've learned not to take each other for granted. Their life has just begun, all over again. They know things others do not. "Do people really make these kind of judgements before going places?"

"Who cares?" Tony laughed. "I'm not researching that. I'd rather have my eyes put out than go to a Club Med. Look at the people who do. My point is not whether the images reflect or create reality, but that they take on a life of their own. They're independent icons, like pictures of saints. No one has the principle experience. Ever."

The couple walked along the beach alone, dignified, but not aloof, and possessed of superior knowledge.

"No," Charles shook his head, agreeing. "It's too easy."

To his right, through the side window, Charles can see a checkerboard flash, black squares separated by mirror-bright silvering: the tarred roofs of cabins and sunlight reflected off water.

"Is that us?" he asks. "Are we there?"

"Not quite. Those are for summer people, the type who arrive with a car full of groceries and a television. That way they can upset the place with their presence the way their absence ruins the place in the winter. The tax base, you see?"

Charles says, "Uhm."

"Up there. That's us. Honest tourists."

Deer Lodge sits at an angle on the top of a steep incline above the lake. The angle is, presumably, to keep its view clear of the cabins lower down, closer to the shore. The lodge appears to be constructed of whole trees in even, horizontal rows, with bark and branches intact but leafless. Deracinated? Charles considers the word. Exfoliated?

Carole shifts down, turns across the dirt road and parks behind the building. The only other vehicle is a sports van, the kind of truck once boxy and clumsy, made angular and threatening by modern principles of aerodynamics. Black tinted-glass windows ribbon its top third like the border of a condolence card. Charles rolls up his own window. The dust raised by Carole's car settles slowly. When he steps from the car, his boots are powdered and, inside them, his feet feel gritty.

"I'll go in and register," Carole says, walking around the front of the car. "I used mister and missus when I made the reservation. You don't mind, do you? It's just that they've known my family for years and years. They might not understand. I'm probably still a little girl to them, like a daughter."

"No, I don't mind," Charles says. "How could I?"

But she's already crossing to the lodge, with or without having heard. After she's turned the corner, he raises each boot separately and stamps it down lightly, like a skunk giving warning before turning its back, tail lifted to release a burning cloud. His feet have the heavy, wooden weight that precedes numbness.

"We may have a small problem," Carole says, although her smile would indicate this can not be so. The rule she lives by is: appear to be exactly where you want to be, in public. She never lets an expression or action betray her private self in the company of strangers; she is afraid of what they might see.

They are in the lodge's dining room. Everywhere there is light. The room's design thrusts it beyond the shadow of trees. Carole can see the only other people—two couples at one table clear across the room—are too distant to overhear, although they take turns glancing over to her and Charles, as if they wished to. The waitress who brought their trout has evidently returned to the kitchen; she is not visible. Charles also smiles, and dips his head towards Carole as if what she has said amuses him and deserves a salute. If the game has rules, it also has rewards.

"And our small problem is?" he asks.

"Champagne."

A middle-aged man appears at Charles' right elbow, having approached from the rear, before Carole could formulate a quick, explanatory sentence. Dartmore. He is carrying a bottle of wine, bucketed in ice, with two fluted glasses held stem-ways between his index and ring fingers. His hands are thick and rough, but he handles the crystal with an assurance both gentle and competent. The man's bearing recalls a phrase Carole read in the operating manual included with Charles' German camera: delicacy of feeling. She has to raise her napkin to her mouth, controlling her gag reflex, before she speaks.

"How lovely," Carole says. "The champagne. Charles, this is our host, Hugh Dartmore. He's the owner of Deer Lodge. Mister Dartmore," she turns directly to address the man with the discreetly confiding tone some adults use in the presence of children. He'll get the point. "This is Charles."

"Hello."

"Yes, of course," Mr. Dartmore says. "I am pleased to meet you. That I was not here earlier was unavoidable. And now you have almost finished your meal."

Charles had scraped his chair away from the table, prepared to stand and offer his hand with the introduction. But the man is busy using his thumbs to ease the cork from the bottle, and Charles alters his crouched posture into a sweeping examination of the room. He notices the other two couples have turned and are facing in his direction, staring openly.

"You have an excellent view, here," he says.

"People are always suggesting improvements," Dartmore says, pouring the champagne with moves precise as a game of chess. "They tell me, 'Hugh, with a little landfill you could put in a deck and have an outdoor terrace'. They tell me where to find old, useless things people have stored in their barns. They tell me many things." He moves the filled glasses, one in front of Charles, one for Carole. "I say this is fine. Now you will have champagne. I cannot drink with my stomach so I will make only the toast. You be good to my Carole and that will be fine, also."

"You won't suggest improvements?" Carole mumbles.

"I think I am," Charles says. This is not a sufficient response; it sounded glib and dismissive rather than agreeable. He feels that he has misunderstood a creed, slighted a benediction. "Thank you," he adds, lost for a more formal phrase. "Thank you, sir."

He sips his wine. Carole merely puts her fingers on the stem of her glass. Both face Dartmore, who brings his hands together at waist level, nods without speaking, then backs away.

"Our small problem," Carole says, after a moment, her voice low.

"He's," Charles pauses, then speaks a rarely used word, "charming. A charming man." He sips his drink. "As for our small problem, I'm afraid I really can't afford a champagne dinner. Do you think we might be able to eat someplace else tomorrow?" This is an awkward confession for Charles, and he is not prepared when Carole covers her mouth and laughs out loud.

"No, we don't pay for the champagne. And you don't pay for anything. This is my trip down memory lane, not yours. I can't allow you to spend your money here. I hope you haven't been worrying about that. I should have made it clear, it's no problem at all." She stops, looking thoughtful. "That would be like selling tickets to my past."

"Nothing wrong with that," Charles says. In mere moments the light into the room has weakened. They are too close to a visible horizon to see the sunset beyond the far shore. Outside, the lake is flat and dull as raw steel. "Hey, I can handle the trout at least. How far back can I go on that?"

Carole doesn't smile. She empties her glass with a series of quick sips before she speaks. Most men would rather have their pants taken off in public than be caught in an act of tenderness; the kissing noises they make at women in the street are deliberately wet, obscene, not to be mistaken for affection.

"I registered us as husband and wife. It was important to me. But I hadn't given it much more thought than that. When Dartmore asked when I, when we, got married, I didn't have a quick answer. He misunderstood my hesitation. Now everyone in this place thinks we're on our honeymoon." She cuts her eyes sideways, towards the other couples, without changing her expression. "Even them, probably."

Now Charles laughs, but he feels a creeping flush of embarrassment as he runs over the last hour in his head. What had he looked like, a newlywed? And Dartmore, what had he thought of Charles, his attention on the view?

"I'm glad I didn't know before," he says. "But now I feel like an actor on opening night, when I was expecting a dress rehearsal."

"I'm sorry. My father always said I couldn't think on my feet." Carole doesn't mention how she misunderstood and thought he meant something dark and Oedipal—she was trampy, meant to do her thinking on her back—her relief when, later, he suggested a public speaking course. Now she says, quickly, "The desserts here are cake and pie. Home cooking."

"Nothing more for me, thanks." He swallows his wine, folds his napkin and pleats the crease between his thumb and first knuckle.

Carole wants to touch his face, the worst possible thing to do.

"We could take the rest of this back to the room." She puts her hand out on the champagne bottle. Charles cradles the bucket in one elbow as he stands. "No," she says. "Don't take his glasses. We have some in our bathroom."

When they are passing the other couples, he hears one of the men say, "Bring back any memories, Phil? Or'd you get it done sober?" One of the women makes shushing noises, but the other squeals, "When he got sobered up later, you mean," before emitting a series of snorts like hammer blows.

Charles smiles in their direction, politely bland and uninvolved.

"'I don't care,'" he quotes. "That was the worst." He is telling Carole the rules for excuses acceptable to his fifth-grade teacher. "'I don't know' was best, and 'I didn't think' was marginal." He is standing in the bathroom, taking the paper-wrapped water glasses out of their sleeves, and talking through the open door. Carole is sitting on the edge of the bed, her crossed legs angling her weight to the arm braced against the tan and orange quilt. The lamplight is dim, reflecting off the wood-panelled walls to give everything a buttery cast. Only in the bathroom are the surfaces white, evenly lit. Charles rinses the glasses and snaps off the light by hitting the switch with his elbow. "I still remember that. The human mind is an impressive instrument. Selective, but impressive." He puts the glasses on the bureau, beside the champagne.

"Carole?"

"What?" She looks up at him, away from the dark panes of the patio doors on the far wall of the room. The room is mirrored in these. "Oh," she says. "I don't know. I didn't think. I don't care."

"You're not *attending.*" Charles mimics the teacher.

"No, sorry." She straightens up to accept the tumbler of champagne. "I was listening, out there. Dartmore is out in his van. We can go now."

"You mean leave? I've unpacked my stuff."

"Not home. We can go to my secret spot." She smooths her skirt behind her as she stands. "I want you to see it."

Charles follows her to the patio doors, then turns back for the bottle of champagne as she slides them open. It's dark outside; even the lake surface is a slick, oily black. He squeezes the bottle to his chest with the hand holding his glass, to lean back and push the door closed. Carol is already ahead of him, walking on an angle away from the path leading to the water. He walks fast, to catch up. The ground under his boots is scrubby and uneven. Her white dress floats in and out of his sight. Diaphanous, he thinks. Ethereal.

"Over here," Carole whispers. "On your left."

She's sitting in a hollow, almost a cave, in the roots of a huge tree. Charles grunts as he swings his leg over a thick, growing thing, steadies himself against the trunk before sliding down its length to sit beside her.

"This is great." He keeps his voice hushed. "We're invisible."

"That's the point of a secret place," Carole whispers. "Nobody knew they were there."

"Agatha Christie?" Charles guesses. "Evan Hunter? Why are we whispering?"

"Because we're scared."

Charles closes his eyes, then touches his lids with the tips of his fingers to discover if he actually has done this. It makes almost no difference. When he opens his eyes, he is slightly more aware of the dim light from the stars.

Straining, he can discern Carole's dress, her face, but this might be an act of imagination.

"What are we scared of?"

"Being afraid," she says, in slightly more than a whisper. "We're scared of being afraid. Can you give me more champagne?"

Charles props her glass between his thighs, sticks two fingers into it, then pours in wine to his knuckles. He passes the glass through the air in front of him until he meets her hand. Then he licks off his fingers and pours more for himself. He sighs, then clears his throat.

Carole reaches out for him. Her hand strikes his shoulder. She lets her palm drop down against his arm, then grips his wrist.

"Is this about me?" he asks.

"No, don't think that." She sips her drink, then swings her glass up at the end of her arm. "Look up." When he moves at her side she settles into the warm space between his arm and his ribcage. His shirt is rough and soft at the same time, like a rash on a sensitive part of the body. "Do you think we're being watched. Is there anybody up there?"

"I'm not sure," Charles says. "The *Columbia* usually is, these days. I really don't know about this specific weekend, though. There must be a way to find out."

"I meant something else." She lifts some of her weight off him. The darkness around her is quiet and still, as though she were wrapped in a blanket.

"Dartmore," she says. Then, "He used to...he was supposed to be giving me swimming lessons, down at the lake?"

Charles tightens his arms around her, and she lets herself be held. She's read that infants cry to be picked up, cuddled, because they have an innate fear of exploding. A twig or pebble is sharp against her ankle, but she focuses her attention on her own story, refusing distractions. While she speaks some of the rage that brought her here flares up with a burning satisfaction: flames at the feet of a martyr. She rushes against this heat to her conclusion.

"My parents would be there, right there, smiling and waving. And, under the water, his hands would be creeping along the edges of my suit, those fingers sliding under wet spandex. Nothing smooth about that, he really had to shove his way in. My parents must have been able to tell what was going on. That was the worst of it, imagining they were complicit."

"They weren't," Charles says. "They didn't know."

"Are you sure?" Carole's elbow digs into his ribs as she raises her glass, swallows. "It's true I never told them. I don't know why I can talk to you. I guess it's because you don't have any values."

"I what?"

"I didn't mean it like that. I meant, you aren't judgemental."

"Oh. Okay, that's better." He's silent. She shouldn't have told him anything. She shouldn't have brought him here, or expected him to understand. But then he says, "My friend Tony, you know Tony? He says that life expectancy increases to maintain a proper ratio between child- and adult-hood. He says it takes something like six adult years to make up for each one spent as a child. It has nothing to do with the discovery of penicillin or vaccines that we live longer, he says, but that there's an organic imperative to recreate the time when we were helpless."

"Tony is such a mystic." Carole pulls herself up to sit beside Charles. There's enough light now, or his eyes have adapted to the darkness, to see that he's facing her. His voice is conversational, but the dark smudges where his eyes are stare at her like dilated pupils. "Do you think he's right?"

"I don't know about right. What I do know is that when you're little, you lack the resources to deal with a big world. Everything has to happen to you on the same level. Can you take this?" He passes her the champagne, makes a fist and beats against his booted calf. "Isn't that why we're here? Because you have the resources now, to deal with Dartmore?"

"Yes, sort of," Carole admits. "No. I thought I could. I wanted to come here and confront him, I was that angry. But on the way here I thought, Well, he'll see that I've survived, that he didn't really touch me. Not really me. And I thought that would be enough, to make him ineffectual."

"And now?"

"Now I don't know. I don't seem to feel anything. Maybe pity, or a kind of sadness, but it's disinterested."

"I could break off the bottle neck and cut up his face," Charles says.

Carole doesn't bother to cover her mouth; she laughs out loud without affectation. From above, at the lodge, she can hear a motor vehicle spinning over gravel and dirt. The sound enters her body as information she can claim or reject.

"Oh, you're a wise one," she says. "How long have you been doing that, seeing through me?"

"I've never done that," he says, pleased she might think he had. "Are we finished here? Can we go back to the room now? I'm starting to feel like we're being watched."

"Astronauts," Carole says, standing. For a second, or less, she imagines she could keep going, up through the air into the pure darkness of space, her body glowing. She leans against a tree for support, then bends to pick up the empty bottle. "You have the glasses? Don't want to litter, those astronauts may have to make an emergency landing."

Carole is in the bathroom, taking off her makeup, washing her face. She's changed out of her dress into a long cotton nightgown. The door is slightly ajar.

In the other room, Charles walks around, touching surfaces with the flat of his hand. He turns on the television and, with a startling crack, the screen fills up with grey and dark grey diagonal lines. He pushes the knob back in, tugs on his earlobe with the same hand. The champagne bottle is in the rubber wastepaper basket, tipped at a festive angle. He picks up the two water glasses.

"Second dibs." Carole comes out of the bathroom, using a white towel to dry the back of her neck, under her hair. "I'm finished in there."

Charles puts the glasses on the edge of the sink, unbuttons his shirt and slips it off. After a moment's hesitation, he drapes it over the hook from which hangs Carole's dress. He bends and steps out of his jeans, leaving them in a pile on the floor, and snaps the waistband of his briefs as he straightens. His elbow hits one of the glasses. It tips and rolls to the edge of the sink. Instinctively, Charles thrusts his pelvis forward, before the glass can drop to the floor. There's a small noise, like book pages turned in a quiet library, and the glass is in two pieces.

"Jesus," he says softly. At the top of his thigh, under the pouch of his underwear, a thin line of blood appears all at once. He turns on the tap, tears off a length of toilet paper. When the bleeding is under control, he steps back into the other room, one hand cupped over his groin.

"Would you look at this?" he asks, standing next to the head of the bed, his crotch in line with Carole's eyes. She turns away, moves across the surface of the bed, taking the pillow her head had been on, flipping the second pillow back to his side.

"Charles, please don't," she says. "Maybe I'm not being fair, but I don't want to think we'd make love and you were using my story as some kind of fantasy."

"What?" Charles sits on the edge of the bed. "Oh, god. Oh, no." But he contents himself, then, with leaning over and kissing her forehead.

"Goodnight," he says. He swings his legs onto the bed, pulls the sheet and quilt over him, reaches out for the brass knob on the base of the lamp. He turns onto his side, one arm bent so his head rests on his hand. He can hear the blood course through his wrist. He is aware of the pulse at the base of his neck, behind his ears, between his legs.

When Carole was speaking, in the hollow of the tree's roots, he had imagined what she was saying: he could see the broad expanse of Dartmore's back, as his shirt was slipped from his shoulders, the exposure of flesh. The scene was neatly bordered by a door frame. The man turned. He looked nothing like Dartmore. Behind him, Charles' brother was facing out of the room. It was not imagination. It was memory.

Charles wills his eyes to stay open. He knows what he will dream.

Charles opened the freezer in the dim light of the basement. He took the orange juice concentrate, because it made a neat package and he could get a lot of the cans into his knapsack. He was seven years old. "Neatness counts" was recently learned.

"Are you ready?" Peter was at the top of the stairs, already dressed for running away, with sneakers and nylon windbreaker.

Charles tip-toed up the wooden stairs to pass the knapsack to his older brother. He slipped his own windbreaker off its hook, folded it over his arm.

"Okay," he said after a quick look around. "Let's go."

They closed the screen door silently behind them and started across the back yard towards the river, Charles shrugging into his jacket as they walked. At the end of the yard, a small and plain dog whined and pulled at its chain. Charles stopped.

"Aren't we going to bring Trixie?"

"Why should we?"

"She'll bark, and Mom will come out."

Charles undid the snap on the dog's collar and Trixie ran ahead to sniff out the direction, then ran back as if the boys' progress were too slow. There were woods at the end of the yard, running the equivalent of a town block before the river. Peter and Charles went through a worn path, with white birch clumps glowing beside them in the pale blue light of early dusk. They came out to the beach and followed the sand towards the setting sun, leaving footprints that marked their way. On their left, the river bank rose steeply in a sandy cliff, and they walked between that and the water. They came to the boat house, a small wooden shack painted dark green, and stopped to play with the boat winch. Charles stood on the spool, his rubber soles gripping the coiled rope, and tried to keep his balance while his brother turned the handle. Trixie ran and snapped at the end of the rope. She slipped over the sand until she was winded. Then she rested, paws under her chin, her tongue drooping out one side of her mouth.

When the sun was completely gone, although there was still light in the air, Peter picked up the knapsack, signalling they were to continue. Trixie followed, on three legs, with the fourth raised and making incomplete short steps that never touched the ground. From the other side of the sand bank, in the hollow that was the rifle range, came the sound of a single shot. The boys stopped, looking up to where the sound seemed to ripple through the air. A man appeared at the top of the bank. His rifle was held low in one elbow. He walked down to them, slowly, and the dog backed over the sand, making rough growling sounds deep in her throat.

"Hey," the man called, when only a few long steps separated him from the boys.

"Hi," Charles answered. He could feel Peter behind him, his brother's unease with strangers.

"Was that you shooting?" Charles asked.

"Sure was. Practicing. There's a rabid owl around here, needs to be destroyed."

"A rabbit-owl?" Charles tried to picture the hybrid, but couldn't imagine anything that needed to be *destroyed.*

"You be careful about your dog, now," the man warned, and Charles understood then.

It was almost dark now, with only a narrow band of light between land and sky, and the boys could barely make out the man in front of them. He took a package of cigarettes from his shirt pocket, shook one out and bent to light it against the wind coming over the water. In the orange flare of the match, with the shadows flickering over his eye sockets and cheek hollows, he was frightening. The boys began, slowly, to walk backwards. Charles watched the lit end of the cigarette, knowing his brother would be watching the gun. Their sneakers crunched over the wet sand, a noise like bones cracking, and they stopped, ten paces from the man.

"Bit late for you boys to be out, isn't it?"

"We're just going home now," Peter said quickly.

"Going this way?" the man asked, turning.

"No, we go this way." Peter turned. Charles turned with

him and they started walking away, then broke into a run and heard the man's voice, loud but indistinct, call after them. Charles turned again and on impulse he ran a few yards back, threw his arms open to the night air and called a ringing, "Goodbye!" The man raised one arm and Charles, breathing hard in the dark, raised his own arm and waved heartily.

"I don't think he's going home, either," Charles said in a clear voice. He moved and almost stepped on Trixie.

"Come on," Peter said.

Charles let his knapsack fall from his shoulder, dragging it by the straps behind him. It left a rounded trough in the deep sand that erased their footprints. The wind rose up, solid and warm, and the sky was mottled with yellow light from the moon. They walked for an hour, or what seemed like an hour. Sand crusting on the soles of their sneakers slowed them down. They had gone this far in the daytime, but it was unfamiliar ground in the dark and they walked carefully. When Charles looked back he could see none of the lights of town. Over the river there was a pale image of another town, pin-points of distant light. Where the bank swept forward to the water in a tangle of small trees and sharp rocks, they could not walk around the point so they crawled up the bank, on all fours in places, until they were at the top, almost five yards over the water. The dog came after them in short hops. She stood at the top, poised, like a darker dog-shape cut from the darkness behind her.

They made a nest in the long grasses by rolling over and over until they had flattened a large circle. Their nylon jackets glowed like snail tracks in the moonlight. They sat across from each other. Trixie was under Charles' arm.

"When are we going to go home?" Charles asked in a whisper. He could hardly remember why they had left.

"Never."

Charles slid his fingers through the dog's fur, to the thicker fur at the neck, groped until he came to the buckle on the leather collar. With deft fingers he pulled the strap through the metal clasp. He flipped the collar through the air with a wild, sidewards toss, and imagined he heard the small splash as it fell into the river. Then he rubbed the dog, briskly, to remove the traces of flattened fur. Trixie whined and moved closer and Charles felt, all at once, lost and tired.

"What are we going to do?" he asked in a weak voice.

"Well, we have food until we find things," Peter answered, then fell into a thoughtful silence. After a moment he spoke, his voice confident. "There's blueberries. You like blueberries, don't you."

"Yeah, I guess so," Charles agreed, unwilling to be enthusiastic. He sat back in the grass, pulled at the ground to make himself comfortable, and curled up with the dog held to his chest. He closed his eyes and tried to remember what his room felt like at night. He thought of the lamp beside his bed and, pressingly, the bathroom just down the hall. He heard his brother move, then the clink of the cans as the knapsack was opened.

"What did you bring?" Peter demanded.

"Orange juice," he answered, too sleepy to be defensive.

"Orange juice. Why?" Peter's voice was loud.

"Because it fit in the knapsack." Charles was awake now, and ready to argue. But his brother yielded, and fell to prying off the spiralled lid of one tin.

"Want some?" Peter asked in a quieter, conciliatory voice. He passed over the can, with its top folded to a sharp edge.

"Thank you," Charles answered with cool reserve. He held the can to his lips, but the drink was slushy and not easily poured. He had to suck to get any of the tart concentrate. He passed the tin back to his brother, making appreciative noises as though it had been just what he wanted. Peter took the can and held it, but didn't try to drink.

"I'm not going home," he spit out suddenly, making Charles sit up quickly. "Not ever. I'm going to stay here forever. Then they'll be sorry."

"What'll we do out here?" Charles asked, torn between his loyalty to his brother and his desire for home.

"I'm going to live in the woods." Peter pushed himself to his feet, the can of orange juice held like a grenade in his hand. With sudden inspiration, he pulled his arm back. "I'll kill the owl!" he swung the can forward in a wide arc, concentrate glugging out in thick splotches, then pitched with a tremendous force. A wild plume of orange struck Charles across the eyes, making them sting and smart, and ran down over his cheeks. Charles wiped at his face with his jacket sleeve, momentarily blinded. His remaining senses acute, he was able to hear something other than the crinkling fabric, more than the deep pitch of his brother's breathing.

"What's that?" he hissed. "Listen."

They froze, listening; sounds like glass breaking, and

running water, and many voices, high and excited.

"It sounds like a party, just under us."

They crawled the short distance to the edge of the bank and peered down. Instead of the party they had imagined—deceived by the diverse noises channelled to them over the smooth surface of the river—there was only one figure. The man with the gun. They could see the base gleam of the barrel propped on a twisted piece of driftwood. The man was striving for a handhold, to climb up to where they were.

Charles felt his arm bend backwards, realized he was holding onto Peter and slowing his escape. He released his grip and ran with, or after, his brother. Charles tumbled once, sprawling helplessly over the earth, refused to stop, ran on his hands and knees until he could stand again, a sandy beard over the sticky orange on his chin. They went through the woods, close to the ground, and threw themselves in with the sandbags behind the targets at the rifle range, pressed themselves into the cold ground there. Charles clutched a handful of the rough burlap. He was small, inconsequential, surrounded by empty air, and he needed to anchor himself to the planet as it spiralled through the vast darkness of space.

After a while Peter rolled carefully onto his side, moved his lips close to Charles' ear and whispered, "Do you think he'll find us?"

Charles only moaned in answer, a deep, low sound, and shook his head violently. He felt something move against his leg, lost control and screamed, one high, shrill note before his brother's hand clamped over his mouth and the dog moved up to his face with the same soft, damp touch.

He sobbed then, in relief or terror, and wanted to be home or dead. Peter moved closer and put one arm over Charles' shoulders to contain his shaking. After a moment, he brought his knees up to kneel beside Charles.

"It's okay," he said quietly. "We'll go home now."

They walked across the range. The woods were quiet. Trixie disappeared into the underbrush, after some elusive prey, but the boys continued without calling to her or slowing their pace.

Only when they stood at the end of the yard, the lawn like a plush carpet before them, only when the house was in front of them, a single light burning on the back porch, only then did they consider having to stand, humble and contrite, before their parents. They went into the garage, instead, by the side door that was never locked. Charles opened the car door and climbed into the back seat. He clutched the wet front of his jeans and was asleep before his brother started the car engine for warmth.

Sometime before sunrise he was taken from the car. And then nothing was the same.

Carole idly wishes she smoked. It would be nice to have something to do, an activity that would suggest she was not doing precisely what she is doing: sitting up in bed and watching Charles sleep. She's taking advantage, of waking first, of the sunlight through the patio doors. His eyebrows are pulled together over his nose, his mouth turned down at the ends. She's seen this expression on him awake, when he's trying to remember the words to one of the country songs he loves—the one about Louise's body being sent home on the mail train—from an album he's worn smooth, grooveless, and cannot replace. Carole likes jazz; the one time she heard this song, on Old Gold radio, she was irritated to find her eyes stinging, her throat sore. He's musically naive.

But, she considers, he did not react to her with horror, or disgust. He has a well of patience she's never appreciated; he may see his life in the simple form taken from the lyrics to such songs, where victims are not complex studies of psychological masochism. Things happen. Things fall apart. Accident means without culpability.

She slides out of the bed, careful not to pull the covers from his body, then crosses to the bathroom, closing the door behind her.

Charles decides to check the dining room first, uncertain he'd be able to find her secret place in the daylight, unescorted. He's relieved to see her at the end of the room, in front of the windows, sitting at an unset table. He doesn't know why—relief—but that's what it feels like.

"I found you gone," he says, sliding into the chair across from her.

"I was walking. For miles, it seemed like." Carole smiles. "I went to all the places I remembered best. And then I said goodbye. To all of it." She stands, holding up one palm. "My purse is still in the room. I should go get it. No, you stay here, keep the table."

Charles looks around the room. He puts his hands flat on

the table, then lifts them off, lowers them into his lap. He runs his little finger over the seam in his jeans, at the top of his thigh. The waitress appears at the kitchen door, moves quickly towards him.

"Breakfast?" she asks, flipping the blue-lined pages of her order book with the eraser end of a newly-sharpened pencil. "Toast and coffee?"

"I'm not sure," Charles says. "I'm just the table hostage. I'm with someone." He sees Carole, back in the room, walking towards him with an unreadable expression on her face. She's not wearing a bra under her pink undershirt top. "I'm with that woman. We haven't decided."

The waitress glances over to Carole, "Her? Does she have a gun?"

"What? Oh, because I said hostage. I see." He notices the waitress is wearing a hairnet, a fine complex of grey lines. "Look, we'll both have coffee, okay?"

The waitress leaves, scuffing the crepe soles of her shoes on the wooden flooring. Carole takes her seat at the table. Her face is flushed.

"What happened to you last night?" she asks, then goes on before he responds. "I went back into the room and the maid was holding up this sheet with a great bloody stain on it. She looked at me and said, 'Surprised you lived through it, missus.'"

Charles makes a loud noise. He brings both hands up to cover his face. His shoulders jerk up and down.

"It's okay," he says, through the trap of his fingers. "I'm laughing." He pulls his hands from his face. "Oh Jesus, how do we get here?" he asks. "How do any of us get to be where we are?"

Outside the window, the trees on the opposite shore meet the sky in an jagged line like the teeth of a giant zipper. Horizon, he thinks. Moon and stars. Sharp edges.

A FEW ACCIDENTS AMONG FRIENDS

Sara was engaged to a famous writer who was killed in a car accident three days before the wedding would have taken place at her parents' home in Rochester, New York. Dave has to keep the truth of this in a separate part of his mind, like a caged animal. The car accident occurred at roughly the same time Princess Grace of Monaco died, the same week, at least, so Dave's memory of the time is dominated by images from a television camera moving close, from the foot of a coffin, to the embalmed nostrils of Her Serene Highness, the most titled woman in the world. A photograph of her lying-in-state appeared, in colour, on the front of the Ottawa paper. The writer was given a brief obituary on page five of the Entertainment section, under a photograph of a Canadian writer with the same last name. The confusion helped Dave keep the real event trapped at a safe remove. That was in September, 1982.

In 1974, for the third time in his life, Dave was a passenger on his college roommate's motorcycle, a Kawasaki 280Z (or so he remembers; he was never passionate about road vehicles, from infancy preferring airplanes). On a clear stretch of road, approaching an intersection, Dave bent his upper body to the left, to be able to look forward around Michael. The broadside of a dull yellow car was sliding towards them with the effortless fluidity of a sailboat on a calm lake. Almost at the moment he decided that this was not possible, that he was suffering a failure of vision, Dave pulled his head back and heard his own bones shatter as he was ripped from the bike. He'd abandoned his ambition to be a stage actor even before he dropped face-down on the highway.

"In my next life," Dave tells Karl, "I'm only going to be friends with people who were orphaned very young and raised in a succession of abusive foster homes." They're on their way to the airport. Sara's flight is due at three-twenty.

"Why not just foster homes?" Karl asks. "Why would they have to be abusive?"

"To guarantee that the kids would turn out cold. Emotionally, I mean. I don't want to know people who're walking around with bits of their lives *hanging* off them."

"I see," Karl says, and he might. He's a professor of psychology at the college Dave graduated from, although they met after that in California at a human-potential workshop Dave now summarizes as "A place to get naked on prime real estate and pretend your problems aren't self-indulgent." They shared a cabin there. Now they share a house in the suburbs of Ottawa. Dave is not especially impressed with this arrangement as serendipitous, or proof of a *small world.* For his first twenty-five years, he never spent more than three years in any one place; he skipped learning his own life was a single story, with a beginning, a middle and an end. Stops and starts, that's what he learned.

"What I'm supposed to do, I think," Dave says, "is hold her at arm's length, then cup one hand under her chin and say, in this deep, sincere voice, 'How *are* you?' I don't know if I can manage that."

"Just be yourself. You've been watching too much television."

"Television?" Dave is offended. He tugs down his raincoat where it's bunched under the shoulder strap. He refuses to wear a winter coat before Christmas and has two more weeks in his Aquascutum. "I'm talking about films, here. Black and white, with subtitles. On television, if you ask a woman how she is, she tells you about the comfort and protection she feels with her new panty liners."

He turns to watch for the sculpture along the Airport Parkway. There's a pile of rusted metal that looks like a piece of farm equipment abandoned in a snowy field. He used to point it out to people, saying, "See, the location of that, essentially trash, makes it Art. It defines the space around it as *field.*" Later he found out the metal construction had been sponsored by the National Capital Commission. If it's still art, he's decided, it's sentimental art, merely self-defining. He's cold-blooded in assessments of culture.

"Protection," he repeats. "I don't even know what that means."

"I'm going to wait here," Karl says, pulling the car into the lane under a sign saying *Arrivals and Pick-up.* "Save the trouble of parking."

"Okay." Dave pats Karl's knee. "Later."

Inside, the airport building has the unique scent Dave loves, a combination of high school corridors, theatre lobbies, and gas stations, suggesting captivity with the possibility of glamorous escape. He checks the terminal display and discovers Sara's flight was early, so he hurries to the baggage claims area. A woman smiles at him. She's wearing a blue coat resembling cunningly shredded blankets. He smiles back, remembering First Class travel. The coat can't be warm, but it is elegant. After a second, he throws his arms around the woman.

"Sara!"

"Me," she says, into his shoulder.

"How—" He pushes her back, holds her at arm's length. "Your hair's different, that coat," he says. He's filled with an immense elation, a feeling like reprieve. This happens in less time that it would take the numbers to change on a liquid quartz wristwatch and, as quickly, becomes gratitude. "You look wonderful."

Karl and Sara are in front of the fireplace. They've started on the duty-free gin that Sara presented, asking, "Who gets the gift for the hostess?" Dave glanced at the bottle, "Mother's ruin? That'd definitely be Karl."

"Not my mother," Karl said. "She thinks gin is low-rent. You know, what you'd serve the char, if you had her in for drinks." He broke the seal on the bottle and added, "Not that one would, of course."

"The woman drinks Manhattans," Dave said. "Whenever she gets away from *the home.*" He waved a hand in front of his face, saying "the home" to italicise the phrase, to suggest more, or less, than *home.*

"She calls it the prison," Karl told Sara.

"It's a fine place," Dave said quickly. He ran cold water into the sink, pointlessly, then closed the tap and wiped his dry hands on a dish towel. "She wasn't looking after herself properly, and she's much better off there. Let's move into the other room. Kitchens are barbaric places for conversations. You may have noticed, they're the usual setting for situation comedies about families. Yes? I rest my case." He took it upon himself to finish the white wine that was served with dinner.

Now he sits in the chair facing the fireplace, with his chin down, watching. Sara is wearing a beaded sweater that looks more like money than would cold cash. With her hair up, and the make-up that's new for her—slashes of plum-colour from cheek to temple—she might be a woman he's never met, but would stop on the street to ask, "Do you know Sara Rogers?" and mean, "Are you her sister?" although his experience has been that family resemblance is over-rated (and he'd resent any comparison with his brother or sister). In 1979, in Rochester, she had shoulder-length hair with a centre part, no visible eyelashes, and an intellectual pallor. She had the ageless, innocent visage of a serious student. Then he remembers her green dress. Slub silk, with a low-cut, square top. Sara's flesh had been squeezed over the fabric in a soft roll, the generous swell of skin once mandatory for movie stars. He thought, then believed, she must be a woman with amazing secrets, and he contrived to be introduced. Tonight, for no reason he can isolate, it is Karl who looks like a stranger to him.

"The executors decided to sell the house," Sara says.

"House?" Dave asks. She lives in an apartment. At least he sends his letters to one.

"I wasn't allowed to claim common-law status, since we'd got a marriage licence. I didn't really have any right to stay there."

"Legal rights," Karl says, nodding. "Family law is a complicated field these days. It's not like when there were rules that everyone understood."

"Oh, sure." Sara looks into her glass, then repeats, "legal rights." Karl cuts his eyes to Dave, who raises his shoulders slightly. After a moment, she says, "I'm going to stay on for my doctorate. It's not perfect, but it's a protected environment. I like the teaching, and I won't have to go out into the real world for a while."

"I never have," Karl says. "At least, not by that criterion. But it's not a bad life, I think."

The weight of the pewter goblet in Dave's hands is real, and vaguely sacramental. The wine makes him feel another weight, the obligation of wisdom or sympathy. Only phrases from country ballads occur to him: *love's not what you get in return, but what you give* and *I'd hold my life in his saving grace.* An unbidden image, of planting his feet and belting out "Colorado," is appalling to him, although his intention would be sincere. When he was immobilized in the hospital, a tape of Elton John's "Daniel" had been an odd comfort. There was consolation in the non-exclusivity of *the scars that don't heal.* No, there was reassurance in the recognition of such an event, the magnitude. Later, hearing the song after some hiatus, Dave realized that Daniel had died and only his body was on the plane. By then, the state of Daniel's health was irrelevant; what mattered was the consequent emotional logic. Dave had heard what he'd needed to hear.

Karl says something about the shortage of tenure track positions, the snail's pace of attrition, and Sara nods as through she's hearing this for the first time. She asks questions to which Karl will have answers. Her gift for unfeigned attention has caused Dave to tell her things he wouldn't share with another living soul. Years from now, two or three, he will find, in an anthology of short stories, a paragraph beginning:

Dave, a sometime painter, sometime artists' model, was what Bud's mother would have called a 'free spirit.' He still had, in his bureau drawer, the polaroids they had taken of each other on their trip to Esalen. Dave had bleached his hair and struck artful poses, his eyes sideways, sly.

But that will be later, when he understands that being used in this way, as inspiration, being transformed in another's imagination—this creation is an act of love, a response to the touching nature of knowing, as much as is possible, more than one self. When Sara calls, apologetic (the story first appeared in an obscure journal, the editor had submitted it to the anthology, she'd expected it to die on the page) his response is, "Well, of course I saw it. What, you think I live in the sticks?" And the flattery will warm him. He will be quite impossible to live with for a while, demanding people look at his eyes, offer their opinions as to relative slyness.

Frozen rain clicks against the windows at the front of the house, facing east. The neighbourhood is quiet, without the sounds of people or cars. There's no through-traffic; box planters from City Works have closed the street, re-defined it as a dead-end. Dave raises one hand to his forehead. The skin over his skull is warmer than his palm. He remains silent. The lights on the Christmas tree blur, then sharpen into five-pointed stars.

In the morning, the city has an icy glaze. Dave stands at the window, as though his presence will assure Karl's safe navigation of the driveway. And it seems to. He waves as the red car moves to the corner and turns.

The small park across the street has a line of silver poplars along one end, separating the space from the high school's playing field. Dave watches some kids—first-period phys ed?—trying to cross-country ski over the smooth surface. They appear and disappear through the tree trunks and he knows, were he closer, he would envy their energy, the effortless gloss of their high spirits and perfect health. Equally, but more shamefully, he would be contemptuous of their matter-of-factness, their conviction of eternities of *now.* If there is a distance greater than that between eighteen and twenty-nine, it's beyond his comprehension, in the manner of black holes in outer space, or the eventual convergence of parallel lines. He doesn't want to know about it. He doesn't need to.

"I didn't think I'd be able to find you. This house goes on forever."

Dave turns. The room is grey, compared to the brightness outside, and it takes him a few seconds to bring Sara into focus. Her features are sleep-blurred, without the sharp definition of cosmetics, and her hair has been flattened on one side. He thinks of kittens in a pet shop window; there's always one sleeping with its tail in the water bowl.

"Actually, no level is more than two rooms deep," he says, holding up his hands at unequal heights to illustrate this. His thumbs, one up, one down, are the stairs. "You have to remember not to move very far in a straight line, or you'll never *get* anywhere."

"I'll keep that in mind." Sara glances at the window, smooths down the lapels of her dressing gown and pulls the sash tight. "This is really a settled place, isn't it? It suits you."

"It does?" Dave looks around. The Christmas tree has displaced the Regency lady-and-gentleman chairs. They've been pulled forward, away from the wall, so there's only a narrow aisle in front of the couch. All the end tables are cluttered with ashtrays, cigarette boxes, silver dishes and trays. He assesses these quickly. They're relics from another era, a time when people 'withdrew' after dinner, left calling cards, offered humbugs to visiting nieces and nephews; the era is known as a time of gracious living by those not involved with its daily maintenance.

"Most of this stuff is Karl's," he says. "And a lot of it came from his mother's apartment, when she moved. It was crazy, that spring, trying to make room. The place wasn't exactly empty to begin with. I always thought of myself as being a rather austere person. When I move, I *go*. There're things of mine from here to Victoria. Like, my Water-Pik is in Calgary."

"You know exactly where?" Sara makes an odd expression, then laughs. "But what, you don't get attached?"

Dave takes a moment to understand what she's heard him say. He turns away, so she won't see his grin, and says, "I just have a tidy mind."

"With a special compartment for loose ends?"

"Well, yes." Dave laughs, delighted at being found out. "Something like that. Something a lot like that."

There's the sound of running water from the downstairs bathroom. After Karl returned from school, Sara had put down her drink and suggested she'd have to get ready before they went out.

"Anything you need?" Dave asked. "I put out towels but, some Vitabath?"

Sara said, "No, that's okay."

"Algemarin?" Dave suggested, starting towards the stairs, animated by the pleasure of being a thoughtful host. He'd had to abandon his plan of showing her the city that afternoon, because of the weather, and needed to provide more than amenities available in a merely adequate hotel. "We have that."

"Really, it's all right," Sara said. "I don't need anything."

Dave, thwarted on his mission, heard his voice rise as he snapped, "Don't be so diffident. Even when you poach a chicken, you don't just sling it bare naked into plain water."

Now Sara is having a shower.

"I'm not sure what *that* was all about," Dave says. "But I think she won."

"She's not like the other people you know." Karl's using the tone of voice Dave considers *professorial.* "I wouldn't have expected—how are you holding up?"

"Sara's special," Dave agrees, then wonders if the comment isn't slightly barbed, like calling someone charming, a word he believes to have a definition barely this side of psychotic. "No," he shakes his head, "she isn't like anyone else I know. Hey, wait a minute, what are you saying about my friends?"

"Well, you know." Karl smiles. "They are rather...."

"Shallow?" Dave finishes. "Listen, that's a gift. It's not everyone who can manage to stick to the surface of things."

"Nor would want to, I shouldn't think."

"Think what?" Sara comes into the room. She's wearing a long skirt, a silk top cut rather like a long-sleeved T-shirt, and a pair of sparkly boots that Dave wouldn't have been surprised to see walking towards a group of sailors. The shower spray has restored the curl to her hair without wetting it into strings and strands. Her make-up radiates energetic good health.

"For god's sake," Dave says, glancing down at his jeans and track shoes. "Now I'll have to change." He gulps down the last of his drink and stands.

"We were discussing personality theory," Karl tells Sara, as Dave starts to leave the room. "Dave takes a unique approach."

"Theory?" Dave turns back. "Is that what you academics call an opinion?"

Half an hour later, in the garage, he says, "Watch this," to Sara.

They're standing on the right side of the car. Karl lets himself into the driver's seat, pulls his seat belt closed, and presses the remote for the garage door opener. He starts the ignition before he leans across to unlock the passenger door.

"You did it again," Dave says, sliding into the front seat. "Don't you think it'd be better to let us in out of the cold before you make yourself comfortable?"

"You're not always waiting," Karl says. "I'm usually alone, and this is my personal routine."

"You could learn a new one."

"It would be against my nature."

"Skinner," Dave points out, "taught pigeons to play ping-pong. That's not exactly *natural.*"

"If you're interested in conditioned responses, you shouldn't be living with a Jungian." Karl steers the car down the drive.

"If interest had anything to do with it, I'd live with an investment banker."

"Are you guys serious?" Sara asks. "I could stay home and watch television."

"After I changed? Don't be ridiculous." Dave glances sideways and Karl winks at him. He twists in the seat to face Sara. "We'll suffer through this together."

"Since we're dressed?" Sara laughs. "Actually, I like having the chance to get decked out. I don't much worry about what I wear to school. I wonder if I'm going to turn into one of those woman professors with the sensible shoes and the too-long skirt?"

"You look very nice," Karl says.

"So do I." Dave presses his knees closed around his hands, palm to palm, and shivers. His raincoat doesn't fit over a sports jacket, however light. He doesn't own a suit, a situation he's proud of and refers to too often. The car heater doesn't have time to be really effective, in the short drive to the restaurant, and the cold causes a familiar ache in the healed fracture site of his leg, where there's a metal plate. His knee makes a terrible noise, like crumpled cellophane, when he swings his legs out of the car. The effort he makes, to stand straight, shortens his breath.

"We'll go ahead," he gasps, and they leave Karl in the parking lot, to find a space.

He and Sara start to cross over to the outside stairway that leads up to the restaurant. At the side of the building, a huge spruce is circled with strands of coloured lights. Reflections of yellow, green and blue dot the white clapboard, the white ground.

"You're limping," she says.

"It's these shoes," he says, pointing down. The shoes are oxblood patent leather, with very thin, very slick soles. He doesn't imagine blaming them will be called into question. "They're not made for walking."

"Same with these boots. We'd better help each other out." Sara puts her arm under his elbow, taking some of his weight before he can lean back, away from her. "You can give me a little support, okay?"

"Sure. I can do that." When they reach the bottom of the stairs, he pulls his arm away and stands with his back to the building to admire the tree for a moment. Then he says, "I went into the store and asked for these. 'Restaurant shoes,' I said, meaning something dressy and not necessarily practical. Like, I'd have them on for no more than four hours at a time and, at that, only when I was getting a drive or taking a cab somewhere. But women wear these things like *appliances* on their feet."

"What can I say?" Sara shrugs in a coyly acquiescent way.

"That I'm right?" Dave suggests. "You could say that."

"Oh, you know everything," Sara says. "And you control thousands of people."

Dave raises one arm and waves in the direction of the parking lot, as if Karl would have forgotten where he was going.

"Here," he calls out, and the word is a pale, wispy shape in the cold air.

There's an office party, three tables over, four men and two women with a slightly greasy look about them, the slickness of too much squeezed into, or out of, a day. A basket of rolls on their table goes untouched after its arrival is greeted with murmurs of protest and one high shriek of horror. Dave is familiar with the conventions of public dining; he has his own, petty, gestures of self-control, self-denial. And to what point? he wonders. Who is deceived? Under our clothes, we're all naked (some of us, he admits, more impressively than others) and hunger is human.

"White wine, very dry," he tells the waitress. "And lots of it."

"What's good?" Sara asks.

"Nothing is bad," Karl says. The waitress clicks her tongue against her teeth and heads off to get the wine. "Nor especially good. It's all a kind of imitation Continental."

"Oh, it's the best place in Ottawa," Dave says. "Have a pork chop or something."

"A pork chop? I spent an hour on the plane, then you take me to your favourite restaurant and suggest I have a pork chop? This is the best place in Ottawa?"

"Dave doesn't mean *best* that way," Karl explains.

"No," Dave shakes his head. "The food has nothing to do with it. I mean, it's the best dining experience in the nation's capital. This is the last place in the city, maybe the world, where women wear hats."

"Hats?"

"Look around." Dave spreads his arms, expansive, in the manner of presenting a gift too large to be handed over. "Hats," he repeats. He watches Sara scan the room, taking note of the elderly women seated at the tables in front of the windows. They are, indeed, hatted. The office party catches her attention. Neither of the women at that table are in hats; they are outfitted in severe, tailored suits, with hair 'done' as an accessory.

"Can you hear those people?" Sara turns back to him. "What are they speaking?"

Dave angles his head, bends at the waist as if he's pulling up one of his socks. The office party conversation comes to him without distortion. He straightens and drops his napkin into his lap.

"French," he says. "Or what passes for it in this town."

"Really?" Sara frowns. "I have three years of college french and I can't understand a word they're saying."

"If they work for the government, which is possible, you wouldn't understand them in english, either," Dave says. *"Hopefully. At this point in time. Prioritize."*

"You shouldn't have gotten him started," Karl says. "He can go on for about a quarter of an hour."

"Time-frame. Cost-wise. Window of opportunity."

"What is he doing?"

"Speaking governmentese. Let's hope he doesn't become bilingual."

"A mutual goal. Cultural mosaic."

"Would you stop?" Sara reaches across the table and slaps his wrist.

"What?" Dave raises his hands to his face, elaborately crosses and uncrosses his eyes. He looks surprised to see her. "Where am I? What happened? Have we eaten yet?"

"He's not easy to live with," Karl says.

"No one is." Sara looks down at her hands. Dave leans forward. Her cuticles are shredded, the nails ragged and painful-looking. She opens her menu again, keeping her fingertips folded under. Her grip is blunt and precarious. "I really don't want a pork chop."

They take a long time to order. The wine is finished and replaced in the process of deciding on the veal. Dave stuffs half of a buttered roll into his mouth and looks around the room. The office party has left; the table was scarcely disturbed by their presence. Two busboys push it closer to its neighbour, straighten the white cloth, then arrange chairs around the two together and begin laying out cutlery, china and glass.

"She's much more alert," Karl is saying. Dave has missed a change in the conversation. "They make sure the residents have a lot of social contact."

"My parents still have each other," Sara says. "But I worry about them getting reclusive together. I'm not sure one would know how to get help if something happened to the other."

"The mailman used to check on her. That was reassuring."

"So, what happened? Was it just a gradual decline?"

"She called, long-distance, to say she'd had an accident," Dave says, interrupting. "At two-thirty in the afternoon. Karl was at school. I said, 'Accident?' and she said, 'I don't think it was a stroke.'" Dave rolls his eyes up to ceiling.

"Was it?" Sara asks Karl.

"No, no." He shakes his head. "She'd tripped on the phone cord and was a little confused."

"So he finds out that evening, when he gets home," Dave says. "And I'm alone all afternoon wondering if the woman's had a stroke. Like, I really *need* this. I didn't even have a number in Toronto I could call. Well, *hers,* of course, but there wasn't much point in that. Language is the first thing to go."

"It must have been awful for you." Sara bends over her plate and cuts a piece of meat into shreds.

"I practically had cramps." Dave laughs, suddenly. "I know it wasn't about me, really, but it was an uncomfortable position to be in."

"Unlike lying on the floor with a sprained ankle." Karl says.

"Well," Dave grins. "She had the phone. She could have ordered Chinese food or something, to fill the time. Szechuan." He looks away, then says, "My god."

The reset table, where the office party was, has been occupied by a group, a family, although there's no father. The mother is a dark-haired, abundantly fleshy woman in a tight black dress. From her right, ringing the table, are her five sons. From about twenty-two to, maybe, eight years old, each is homelier than the last, and they are all in dark suits with white shirts. The eldest has fairly regular features, but there's a crescent of white above his ear, showing through the black hair. Dave remembers a movie where the heroine had been kicked in the head by a pony on her tenth birthday. Later, the girl found love in Florence or someplace. If the movie were re-made, he thinks, the location would have to be changed to a place where Americans could still be considered innocent. No place occurs to him.

At the end of the table, and 'birthday' is still on Dave's mind, the daughter, sixteen today, is a red-head with pale, freckled skin. She's wearing a green dress that looks too stiff to be *retro* in the real sense, but it's a style that makes Dave think of his sister's clothes in the late Fifties, or the fashions still worn by the Queen of England. And—this is too perfect to be true, Dave's hands drop to his lap—she has a tiara in her hair. Rhinestones glitter brightly in the moderate, artificial light.

"Don't be too obvious," Dave says in a low voice. "But check out that table." He tips his head in the direction. Sara and Karl shift and turn, then look back at Dave. "This is terrific," he says, clutching his thighs. "This is going to break my heart."

"Maybe you shouldn't watch," Sara suggests. "I could move my chair to block your view." She hunches her shoulders and leans to the side.

"No, no," Dave shakes his head. "Don't get in my way. I mean, what else is a heart *for?*"

"His two emotional states," from Karl. "'It breaks my heart' and 'It makes me laugh.'"

"Nothing in between?"

"I'm a little more complex than that," Dave protests. "You left out, 'It makes me weak' and 'I don't have time for it.'"

Sara glances, quickly, over her shoulder, and asks, "Shouldn't this one be an 'It makes me laugh'?"

"Well, wait a bit. I'll keep you informed." Dave puts his hands over the table, on either side of the plate. He picks up his fork. "What were we talking about?"

"Mothers," Karl says.

"Don't get me started on mothers," Dave warns. "It's too close to Christmas."

"Are you going home for the holidays?" Sara asks.

"Home? What's that? No, of course not." Dave exaggerates a shudder. "I'll do what I do every year, stay up late and hope 'Silent Night, Lonely Night' is on television."

"That's surprising," Sara says. "It's not what I would have thought you'd be doing at all."

"Oh, I watch *some* television," he says. "Everyone does, it's not so surprising."

"I meant," she starts. "Never mind."

Dave cuts his eyes to the other table. "They're all having the same thing," he announces. "I think it's the chicken. I wonder if they ordered it in advance?"

"I'll be going to my cousin's farm." Karl tells Sara about the traditional family dinner they have, starts to itemize the eccentricities of his relations. Dave drifts in and out of the conversation, his attention at the next table. The mother's hair must be dyed; the black is so dark as to be vulgar. He decides she's a wonderful woman, misunderstood by her neighbours, but loved by her children, who hardly remember their father. How could they, really, with the youngest not even born? But he came early, and was healthy, thank God. She was afraid she'd lose the baby; she might have lost her mind, with grief.

Dave has to do some backward counting, working out the ages of the older kids, to determine their probable responses to a new brother. He insists on coffee and brandy, to extend the time, after their plates are cleared away.

"I might have to close this place," he says. "I can't leave until I see what she gets."

"For Christmas?" Sara inches her chair around. Karl, with a sigh, also turns. "Why would she get her presents now?"

"It's her birthday," Dave says. "Sweet Sixteen. I'm betting on a wristwatch."

"She does look about sixteen," Karl agrees.

"She is, she is. Trust me."

A waitress backs through the door from the kitchen with a tray almost the size of one of the tables. This is ringed with glasses.

"Apple juice." Dave is ecstatic. "There'll be a toast." He clutches his snifter of brandy, to be ready. The waitress serves the birthday girl and her mother first, then circles the table, serving the boys. At some signal from the mother, the son with the hair reaches under the table and comes up with two wrapped packages. The mother leans towards the son and whispers something.

"She can't remember which one is the camera," Dave informs Karl and Sara. "So it can be opened first? This is killing me."

"It is, isn't it?" Sara smiles at him and Dave brings his teeth down over his lower lip, not quite biting. "You're really excited."

"This is *everything,*" he says. "Everything."

"I'll be plucked," Karl says. "A camera."

Dave turns back to the table. The birthday girl has handed a Kodak to her brother, who is bent over, loading the film. Dave squints, but he can't tell if it's a 110 or disk cartridge.

"Now he can get a picture of her opening the wristwatch."

But, first, there's a picture of the toast. All the little boys hold up their glasses of juice. The eldest says, "Cheese," just loudly enough for Dave to hear, and he raises his brandy.

"Cheese."

Sara raises her own snifter, touches it to his. Karl clinks his against hers, then to Dave's, who says, through his teeth, "I didn't see the flash."

There's some trouble with the camera. Dave feels a familiar, sinking sensation. Something has gone out of control. Everything might be ruined.

The son looks up and Dave looks away quickly. When he turns back, the waitress has taken the camera. She's standing at the end of the table, calm and resolute, waving one hand to indicate the mother should stand beside the birthday girl, who is picking, very delicately, at the wrapping of the second package. Seconds crawl by. Karl and Sara are now turned, staring openly. The girl holds up a wristwatch by its shiny black strap. A flashbulb pops and the tiara catches the light, splinters it, shining like shook foil. Light travels at one hundred and eighty thousand miles per second. In less time than it takes Dave to register the halo, the wave/particle is past him, through the window, and on its way to Alpha Centauri, never to return to earth. Never, at least, during the lifetime of anyone now on the planet.

"A camera and a watch." Karl is incredulous. "How did you know?"

"I know everything," Dave says. "And I control thousands of people." He presses one hand into the centre of his chest, making a cage of flesh and bone over his heart. "It was worth waiting for, wasn't it?"

"It was lovely," Sara says. Her voice is almost a whisper.

"It's the best restaurant in Ottawa, Dave says." Karl doesn't sound convinced.

"Let me scoop this." Sara reaches for the bill. "No," she shakes her head when Karl starts to protest. "I want to. I can break in my new AmEx." Her purse is an oddly-shaped scrap of quilted fabric, no larger than a duckling. When she pokes her hand into it, to reach the credit card, the large diamond of her engagement ring snags the lining. Sara twists her wrist impatiently, and there's a sound like the popping of a twig underfoot. Dave's mouth has opened slightly, and he inhales silently through parted lips. His gums are dry. Sara drops the purse onto the table and spreads her fingers. "What I should do, I think," she says, "is wear gloves all the time. Isn't that the first rule of estate planning, cover your assets?"

Dave reaches over the table and puts his hand on Karl's wrist. He moves his thumb in a short arc and says, "I think it's time to go. We won't know if we had a good time until it's over."

CONTACTS

Looking directly forward from the top of the stairs, Wayne can see Angela in the bathroom. She's sitting in the middle of the tub, her back rounded and pink, with an expression of intense concentration focused above the taps on the far wall. Her hair is twisted up, to keep it dry, but a strand has loosened and curls down the side of her neck. An epaulette of bubblebath dots one shoulder. She doesn't look anything like a child; her plump eleven-year-old body appears through the steam like a voluptuous woman's. Wayne, helplessly, feels nudged by an emotion inappropriate for a father. He's been taken by surprise.

He steps down, the tendon behind his ankle straining to keep him level, his heel overhanging the shallow flat into empty air, and turns back to the staircase landing, the sole of his sneaker squeaking. If his daughter called to him now—"Dad?"—he'd quick-step all the way to the bottom of the stairs before calling back, "Yes, Angel?" with his voice made distant by the slight echo of the stairwell, carrying sound upward like a chimney.

It's cold outside, but not that cold, a little below freezing. The air in the house is over-heated, too dry for him to be wearing his contact lenses. He presses the tips of his fingers into his eyebrows, against the ridge of bone. Touching his eyelids would make his discomfort worse, would increase the gritty, cat-tongue scrape of the lenses. Even rapid blinking doesn't help. His whole body is starting to feel dried-out, mummified.

"She's pruning," Wayne says, running cold water from the kitchen tap, over his hands first, then leaning down to splash his face. "I send my little girl to her bath and I'm going to get back a big bag of wrinkles."

"It'll be good for her, a long soak after the ride, relaxes the muscles." Dorothy takes the tea towel from his hands before he can pat his face with it. "Get a paper towel. This's for dishes. I raised you to know the proper use for things."

"You always said not to waste them," Wayne says, carefully tearing off one towel along its perforated edge. "Trees died, you said."

"They've grown more since then, I'm sure." Dorothy shakes out the tea towel and, holding it by the corners, lets it fold over the handle of the oven. "I don't know where I thought *cotton* came from."

"You can use it again and again," he points out. "I think that's the point, that it can be laundered."

"That I could wash it, you mean. We never sent anything out. Only the drapes until that one time, when they came back streaky. And us living like the Lindens for two weeks, with nothing on the windows."

"I remember that," Wayne laughs. "We practically had to sleep in our clothes in case the neighbours looked in and saw us in our pyjamas after eight in the morning." He balls the damp paper and drops it into the plastic bin under the sink. With a big pot of water boiling for the lasagna noodles, the kitchen air has stopped drying out his eyes, but his lenses still feel rough, the skin of his face pulled tight. He steps out into the hall. "Are you about finished, Angelfish?" he calls. "Daddy wants to use the bathroom."

"I'm not *in* the bathroom. I'm changing in *this* room."

"O-*kay.*"

Angela is in his brother's room. The door is closed, the way it always was when Michael lived at home. Wayne would be slightly taken aback to see the door open, with the room occupied.

In his own room, the few changes give the room an impersonal air. It might as well be an hotel. There is a new lamp by the bed, and his desk has been moved under the window to serve as a table for the sewing machine. A folding chair from the bridge set is pushed into the knee hole.

But the bed is in the same place, covered with the same quilted spread. At the foot, his suitcase is unzipped and folded open, all the contents laid out as though ready to be transferred to the dresser. He takes his pigskin shaving kit into the bathroom, puts his contact lenses in a plastic tray of solution, clips down the hinged lids marked L and R, then slides on the old pair of glasses he keeps for an emergency.

"Whoa!"

Everything has moved a half-inch to the left. For a moment, Wayne thinks he's about to fall down. Instead, he grips the edge of the sink and leans forward, closer to the mirror. He's made a mistake in packing. The glasses he has on are from his next-to-last prescription—the frames are almost the same as the ones he should have brought with him, only the strength of the correction is just noticeably different. The world he perceives is not so much blurred or out-of-focus as in the wrong place. Edges are still clear. He holds up one hand, as a test, and his own fingers and thumb seem to come at his face too quickly; he has to fight the instinct to turn away, to duck.

Half-way down the stairs he stops, feeling light-headed, the way he does after he has his teeth cleaned; he needs a few minutes to become entirely himself again after sacrificing his attention to an outside sensation. He nods slowly and the steps in front of him arc wildly. His arm goes up for protection and he drops, knees bent, so he is sitting in the middle of the staircase. After eight-and-a-half hours of driving, with only one stop for burgers and four other stops for a Ladies, his ankles and calves are contracted. They resist him when he rotates his feet, stretches his legs. He can hear his mother and daughter in the kitchen.

"Separate the strips first, and then put one layer over the bottom of the pan," Dorothy says. "Then I'll put in the meat sauce, a little sprinkle of cheese, and you can do another layer."

"They don't fit," Angela says. "They're too short to go

longways, and too long to go sideways."

"So they are. I haven't made this in years, I can't remember what I used to use." There's a loose rattling, a cupboard drawer opening and closing, followed by the unmistakable sound of the drawer under the stove being pulled open, pushed shut. "It was white, I think, maybe with little mushrooms on the sides. I don't know where it could have gone to."

Wayne leans back, his elbows two steps above his butt. His mother will be wearing an apron tied around her waist, a body part now identifiable in that, seen from the front, it is not her bosom or her legs. From the back, her torso looks like a pillow on posts. Angela is probably in jeans and a T-shirt, white with a vaguely rude slogan printed on it. The roundness of her face and her shoulders, the smooth swell of her tummy—the softness these suggest will vanish as she moves about with the confidence of an athlete. Her growth spurt is in front of her. She is nearly as tall as his mother, but she isn't awkward yet.

"My girl," he thinks. Then, with a sentimental desire for inclusion, he changes the thought. "Two-thirds of my women." He wishes Marlene were here. He'd be able to see his life moving in three directions: backwards, sideways and forwards—mother, wife, and daughter. He decides he'll call her at her friend's place, after dinner, although they agreed phoning wasn't necessary until he arrived at the new house. The decision pleases him. He's almost bounding as he enters the kitchen.

"They're slippery," Angela is saying. "I can't get them to lie still."

"Maybe that's not the best way." Dorothy moves to her side. Her shoulders block Wayne's view. "Like—oh!"

"Shit, Gran, you're *bleeding.*"

"What is it?" Wayne says. "Tell me what to do."

"It's nothing." Dorothy puts the end of her thumb into her mouth.

"She cut herself." Angela's face is red, flushed with the heat. Wayne pulls her into his chest, stooping, and puts his hand on her forehead, the same temperature as his palm. Since she was a toddler, the only times she's been feverish were with routine illnesses, the ones she called "chicken pops" and "weasels."

Dorothy holds out her thumb. "A scratch," she says, before running cold water over her hand. "There," she turns off the tap. "All better. I should have thought of this right away; we'll use scissors." She slides open the top drawer and rummages through a tangle of silvery-blue stainless steel. The baby spoon he inherited from his brother is in there. A gift for the first-born, engraved *Michael.*

Wayne cups Angela's elbows in his hands, pulls her arms out from her sides like fins.

"Angelwings," he says, "why don't you go and watch some television?"

"But I'm *helping.* Gran *said.*" She squirms out of his arms. "We're making *lasagna.*"

"Go along. We're just about done, anyway." Dorothy waves the scissors. "I'm almost ready to pop this in the oven. Why don't you set the table? Everything's in the buffet. We'll be ready in an hour or so."

"Forks on the left," Wayne whispers, pointing to her

hand, "knives on the right." He watches his daughter leave the room. Her T-shirt says: *Spend to the end.* He has no idea what it means, but he can't come up with any impolite associations and is relieved. One time he picked her up after school (going right to her classroom at three o'clock rather than be seen hanging around a schoolyard) and her T had a large picture of a lion on the front, with the slogan: *Big Cats Can Be Dangerous.* He chatted with her teacher for a few minutes, feeling like a responsible father until Angela started down the hall. Over a picture of a kitten, the back of her shirt declared: *A Little Pussy Never Hurt Anyone.* His underarms drained like a squeezed sponge and he gaped at the teacher, trying to think of any reasonable explanation he could make that wouldn't implicate him in such deliberate coarseness. Her gaze, in return, was level and unembarrassed and he saw how young she was. Her eyelids were pewter, her short fingernails equally metallic. Wayne wondered about the other kids in the class—who were their parents? Should he let them into the house?

After Angela was in bed, he and Marlene had hissed at each other—"What could you have been *thinking?*" "It's *you* who has the dirty mind, she just liked the pictures." "You mean, strange men are looking at my daughter and thinking, 'That little girl is an animal lover'?"—and the T-shirt vanished into the same void that had swallowed Strawberry Shortcake. One year earlier? Two?

Try as he might, Wayne couldn't *not* think of the phrase "training bra."

"I know one little girl who's getting over-tired," Dorothy says. "She's starting to whine."

"Sure, she's tired. It's been a long day for her."

"Well, that's no excuse for bad language. I wouldn't put up with it from you or your brother." She turns and stares at him. Wayne can't tell if it's the heat or his glasses, or maybe her age, but her skin is blotchy and over-coloured. He has trouble remembering what Angela said.

"Oh, *that,*" he says, after some thought. "I guess it just slipped out. She wasn't thinking, nattering on the way she does when she gets excited. I mean, she was worried about you hurting yourself."

"And I appreciate her concern. It's just an observation I was making. I wouldn't say anything to her on my own." She fixes him with a look and turns to run tap water into the sink, swishing a sponge over the dull stainless steel. "I wouldn't ask her where she learned those words."

"What *words?* One. One word." Wayne catches himself before adding, "Jesus!" Instead, he says, "It's pretty mild, you know. I hear a lot worse from kids on the street."

"Other people's children," Dorothy sniffs. "I wouldn't compare."

"But you just did," Wayne says. "You compared her to me at that age. Like the world hasn't changed in the last twenty-five years."

"I didn't say that. I'm not in the dark about all the things that have changed, but not the importance of raising a young girl to be a lady."

"Actually, these days, girls grow up to be women."

Wayne pushes his fingers through his hair, knocking his glasses askew. Righting them on his nose, he asks, "Isn't it awfully warm in here? Can't we turn down the heat?"

"It's fine for me. I was never warm enough for the forty-three years I lived with your father, and I swore I'd never be cold again. I don't smoke or drink, and I can't remember the last time I bought a pair of shoes, so I think if I want to spend my money on heat, that's my right." Dorothy opens the oven door and slides in the pan of lasagna. The blast of warm air raises her hair at the temples, lightly, like feathers. She doesn't let the door bang shut the way Marlene does, she keeps her hand on the handle.

"Oh. Well, then." Wayne starts to back out of the room. "I'm glad we had this little talk," he says, but not very loudly. More of a whisper.

On her knees before the television, Angela is moving one hand up and down over the panel above the speaker's plastic vent. Her thumb moves in brisk, short arcs like she's counting a large number of bills.

"Not so close, move back a bit," Wayne says automatically. In the blue light, he reads the front of her shirt: *Shop till You Drop.* Then, hearing himself, he shakes his head and makes a click-sound with his tongue against his back teeth. "What're you watching?"

"I *thought* it was videos, but when the news came on it was still in black and white. I think it's the tint or brightness, but I can't find the controls."

"Well, no, Angela. That's a black-and-white set."

His daughter turns a smooth, moon-face towards him and he thinks—he should have known this before—it is possible for a living, human face to have no expression at all. He can't imagine what his own looks like at this moment.

Before dinner, Wayne goes out to the garage, through the door off the kitchen, looking for an extension cord long enough to reach the rented van so he can plug in the block heater. The temperature might drop overnight.

His father's car is gone. Wayne takes a moment to remember Michael offered to handle the sale of it. Neither of them wanted to drive a beige car nearly eighteen feet long, almost seven feet wide. There is a patch on the floor, dark with spilled oil and leaked fluids, marking a space almost the size of a bathroom.

In his stocking feet, he can feel the warmth of the concrete surface. The garage absorbed enough heat through the kitchen wall to be comfortable. More comfortable than the house, in fact. The edges of the roller door are sealed with rubber flanges but, at the top, where the mechanism for opening and closing is attached to the ceiling, there's a thin strip of visible outside light.

He takes a deep breath, and calls it fresh air, before setting to work untangling fifty feet of orange cord, weaving the black plug and socket ends through one loop after another.

"In this house, we eat what's put in front of us."

"G.H.F." Wayne mumbles, the shorthand he and Michael shared, meaning God's Holy Food. Louder, he says, “You like lasagna, Angel. You eat it at home.”

“Mom’s isn’t all red like this.” Her plate is covered with small strips of noodle sliced across with the edge of her fork. Meat sauce creates a lumpy terrain around the paths and trails of flattened pasta. “It looks like it’s *bleeding.*”

“That’s just tomato, hon.” But, since she said it, Wayne notices his own plate looks like exposed guts, clots of blood. He holds his eyes open very wide, then blinks rapidly. The illusion remains. “Well, there’s some ice cream in the freezer, would you like that instead?”

“If it’s vanilla.”

“I think it is, Angelcake.” Wayne stands and takes her plate. His mother has rearranged the dining room since he lived at home, so he isn’t sure if she put him at the head of the table or the foot. He touches his free hand to his mother’s shoulder as he passes, and says, “We’re probably a little queasy from all the driving. It’s not that this isn’t good.”

“I wish you could have said something earlier,” Dorothy says. “Now I’ll be eating this for the rest of the week.”

“You could freeze some. I bet it’d keep for a year.” Wayne raises his voice, to be heard from the kitchen. On the counter by the sink, the leftover amount in the pan looks—he considers—*institutional,* as though she’d planned on more than a family dinner. A family reunion maybe.

“Save it for company,” he shouts, then feels foolish for being so loud when he’s in a room by himself. “Or get a dog,” he whispers, and his mother yells, “What?”

“I said, This is *good.* The ice cream. Are you going to have some?”

"If there's enough," she calls back. "Serve yourselves first."

Wayne bangs the carton down on the counter, yanks the top drawer open so roughly he has to hold it with both hands and re-centre the nylon wheel in its steel track. He breathes through his nose the way he learned to at Lamaze and a small part of his brain tells him he is being irrational, but he's furious all the same. Had he not gotten off the highway here, had he kept going another hundred and fifty miles, he and Angela could be having western sandwiches and french fries in some anonymous motel coffee shop. They'd be that much closer to the new house, the town where he starts his new job in a week, the office where he'll return the U-Haul. They'd be somewhere, anywhere, where he was in charge. Instead, he's spooning house brand ice cream into melmac bowls that vaguely smell of bleach, probably ruining his eyes with these out-dated specs and his whole body feels like it's turning to ashes. Instead, his daughter is cranky and over-tired, about to go to bed hungry and miserable. She probably hates him.

In his fist, the shank of the spoon bends backwards, its edge refusing to cut through the ice-cream. Wiggling it back and forth until it's free, Wayne looks at the curved metal, holds it up to his forehead like a mentalist, and, fierce with concentration, says, "Straighten out. Stop being bent out of shape."

In the dining room, Angela has moved out of her chair and over to her grandmother's. She's too big to fit in her lap, so she's between her knees and draped across her chest. Her head is on Dorothy's shoulder, her eyes closed, and she's breathing through her mouth, fast asleep.

"Shh," Dorothy warns, lifting a finger to her lips. "The poor little lamb is just exhausted. If you'll finish clearing the table, I'll carry her up to bed."

Wayne puts the two bowls down on the table, carefully, so they don't click. He tries to imagine his mother attempting to carry his daughter up the stairs. It'd be like him lifting Michael; she'd have to sling Angela over her shoulder in a fireman's carry. Her legs would bow out like a bull terrier's.

There's time enough for Wayne to say, "I'll do it," so he stays where he is, silent.

Three steps north, three steps south, and Wayne has covered the length of his bedroom. It's too early for him to be asleep, but too late to do anything that might disturb the silence of the house. He drops onto the bed and peels off his socks. The raised pattern on his feet matches the ribbed wool that he balls up and tosses into his suitcase. When he leans back, his head hits the wall with an alarming thump and he waits for someone to call out, to ask what happened. When no one does, he gets up and goes across the hall.

Angela has kicked off her blankets, only the sheet is pulled up to her waist. Her pyjama top is twisted, exposing little birds of skin between the buttons. He kneels beside her bed, meaning to cover her shoulders, but decides her body will know how to keep itself comfortable. With his head tipped towards her face, he listens to her breathing. She isn't quite *honking,* but there is something adenoidal about the sound she makes. A slick feeling on his lower lip tells him his own mouth is open. He stands up and swallows, then goes downstairs, toward the light from the front porch, visible though the door's glass panes.

The phone cord stretches enough for him to be able to sit on the floor of the hall closet, the way he used to when he was in high school and every call was, if not top secret, demanding of privacy. A pair of rubber overshoes have to be pushed to the side, coats slid farther down so they don't cover his head and shoulders. He takes up more room now than then. By leaving the door ajar he can see well enough to dial. While the call completes itself in clicks and whirrs, he wonders what Angela would make of the rotary dial—would she poke through the open holes to push down on the printed numbers? How many times before she either caught on or gave up?

"Leanne? It's Wayne." There is a silence, while he waits for her to let Marlene know it's him. He presses the phone against his ear and narrows his eyes, aware of the unfamiliar stem of his glasses against his temple. The silence is actually a hiss; he hasn't been disconnected. "Hello?"

"Wayne?" Still Leanne. "Is something wrong? You're not supposed to be there until Monday."

"No, no, nothing's wrong. I'm not there yet. I'm here, at my mother's. Everything's on schedule."

"I *wondered.* I mean, anything's possible." Before he can restate his assurance that everything is all right, she talks on. "At your *mother's.* God, that must be a trip. Two minutes on the phone, maximum, with mine, and I'm about fourteen years old. Maybe younger. Talk about getting your buttons pushed. I mean, when I was losing all that weight, every time I'd call her, I'd have to list everything I'd eaten for the last week. And she'd *disapprove.* 'Oh, you shouldn't have had popcorn.' I was, like, 'Blow it, lady, *I'm* the one taking off thirty-five pounds.' And she's no sylph, let me tell you. Gravy on every piece of meat that crosses her lips, she might as well just inject it. No wonder I was such a porker, with her stuffing me like I was some sort of prize pig during my formative years. Well, I *was.* A real prize pig. No one goes to her junior prom in a size eighteen, you don't even get asked. Christ, when I think about being at her mercy that way, it's no wonder I was scared to get close to anyone else. If your own mother gives you the slow suicide, who can you trust?"

Wayne switches the phone to his other ear. Overhead, there's a tinkling of empty hangers. A woolly coat seems to have moved itself back along the pole. A sleeve touches his face. He says, "Uhm?"

"Would you listen to me? I'm going on and on. It's different for guys, isn't it? You've probably got all kinds of shit to work out with your father."

"He's dead."

"What?"

"Dead," Wayne repeats. "He died a year after he retired. Almost to the day, actually."

"God, that's right. Marlene told me. She said she hoped it didn't run in the family, investing your whole life in your job like it was that important. Would you listen to me? Sorry, I wasn't thinking."

"It's okay. Is she there?"

"Who?"

"Marlene. My wife."

"Oh, right. I mean, you weren't calling *me.*" Leanne laughs. "Not on a Friday night. Unless you've started selling vacuum cleaners or insurance. In that case, I'm sure there's lots of guys who'd give you my number."

"Can you put her on?"

"Well, I can't, really. She's not here."

"Not there?" Wayne kicks his feet out, knocking open the door. The hall light falls on him distorted by the closet's hanging contents, as mottled as summer shade under a linden tree. In front of him, his legs move out of focus. "What do you mean, not there?"

"She went out with some people from the office. You know, for her last day there."

"Oh. Oh, yeah." Wayne swings the curled cord, from the receiver to phone, between his legs, so it touches one knee, then the other. Little nudges. He moves his legs farther apart. "Did she say who all was going?"

"Marita, I guess. And Janice. Everyone from Sales, Tom and Eddie and everyone."

"Tom? Tom Gow?"

"That's him."

"Tom Gow," Wayne says slowly, "has hair on the backs of his hands."

"It's true. He *does.* Like little monkey paws. But it's blonde, you can hardly see it in the summer."

"This is February."

"So," Leanne giggles, "maybe he's wearing gloves."

"Jesus," Wayne says, not into the phone. He pushes his

glasses up on forehead. "Did she say when she'd be back?"

"I don't know, midnight? Wait, it's already after that now, isn't it? Anyway, I'm not waiting up for her. She said they were going to the Talisman."

The Talisman doesn't have real food, Wayne remembers. Only chicken wings, nachos, stuffed mushrooms, things like that, from five until seven. Later in the evening, the waitresses only serve drinks. Half-naked. It's not the kind of place a woman would go to, or stay in, by herself. Or with other women.

"Listen," he says. "Maybe it would be best if you didn't tell her I called. I mean, she won't believe you if you say it was about nothing, just to talk, so she'll worry. And if she calls here, my mother will have a heart attack. She always thinks phone calls after eight are bad news. Yes," his voices takes on some authority. "Yes, I don't think you should tell her I called." And, to clinch her complicity, he adds, "You know how mothers are."

"God, right," Leanne says, and Wayne hangs up quickly, not to hear another word come out of her mouth.

The driveway stings against his bare feet. Wayne is in the dark as he works the cotter pin on the van's wide back doors. There is no moon. When a car goes by on the street, he freezes as though he were doing something wrong, his shadow larger than life in front of him, and the pin is suddenly free in his hand. Inside the door, exactly where he put them last, the three sleeping bags are humped together. He has to make two trips, to get them through the house and into the garage (the roller door rumbles directly under his mother's bedroom and he doesn't want to wake her). By staying close to the house wall, he avoids the patch of stained floor. Unzipped all the way around, one sleeping bag makes a pad for the other two, which he arranges so they open on opposite sides. As a thoughtful touch, he folds back the corners, exposing red triangles of soft flannel.

"Angelcake, come on." He shakes her shoulder. Her hair is damply plastered to her forehead, and her breathing is shallow. "Come on, now."

"Already?" she whimpers, raising her head. "It's dark."

"No, it's not morning. We're going to move where it's cooler."

"Okay." Her head drops back onto the pillow and her body goes limp under his hand. She's asleep again.

"Angel?"

Finally, he has to slide one arm under her and haul her off the bed, so she's standing, although most of her weight is tipped back against his stomach. He tugs down her pyjama top and tucks it in, keeping his hand between her skin and the elastic waist of the bottoms, so it doesn't snap. By circling her chest with his arms and bending his knees behind hers to push her legs forward, he gets her to walk. At the top of the stairs he asks, "Are you going to help me here?"

"In a sec." she says. "I'm not all the way awake yet."

It is only a few minutes before they're down the stairs and through the kitchen. Angela blinks in the harsh light of the garage, takes in the sleeping bags on the floor and turns to him.

"What are we doing?"

"It's cooler. Can't you feel it? Here, you hop in this one."

Once she gets herself snuggled in, he turns off the overhead light. There's enough illumination through the crack at the top of the door for him to make his way to his side. Either the moon has come out, or the door is in a direct line with a streetlight. He unbuckles and pulls off his belt, rolls it into a drum and puts his glasses inside on the floor, so he'll be able to find them easily. Then he slides into his sleeping bag, reaching out to pull the zipper closed, brings his arms into his side and uses his shoulders like flippers to work the bag up to his neck.

"This's great," he says. "Comfy?"

"I'm awake now."

"Well, so am I. But we'll be asleep soon." Wayne crosses his arms over his chest, but the position seems too final. He slides his hands lower.

"Dad?"

"Uh-huh?"

"Are you going to wear your glasses tomorrow?"

"Maybe until we leave. I'll have to see. Why?"

"They make you look sharp."

"They do?" Wayne grins. "I didn't know you guys still said that. So, you think your old man looks cool?"

"No, *sharp,*" she corrects. "They make you look pointy."

"Pointy? Okay, hon, no glasses tomorrow."

"Tomorrow." Angela sighs. "Is that when we'll be at the new house?"

"No, no. Come on, you know that. Tomorrow is more

driving. But we can stop for lunch, any place you see that you like. Then tomorrow night we can stay in a motel. There'll be a colour TV there, probably with cable. Won't that be nice?"

"Yeah."

"And then, the day after that, we'll be in the mountains, mostly. You'll never forget the Rockies. Where we're staying, Sunday night, you should be able to see bighorn sheep. Maybe a bear."

"Bears *hibernate.*" Angela yawns. "And then we'll be home?"

"Did I say Monday yet? We've got a long way to go." Wayne turns to face her. The sleeping bag makes a slippery nylon sound. "One more day after that, and then we'll be there."

"And then Mom will be home?"

"On Monday, while we're driving the last leg, Mommy will be helping the movers with all the rest of our stuff. That's why she's not here now." Wayne squints in the direction of his daughter. All he can see is blotches of black and grey. "But we'll be able to move right in, with what we've got in the van. And then she'll fly out, on the very next plane, to come and be with us."

"Is that it?"

"That's all I've got planned, Angel. What else were you expecting?"

"I just wondered." Her voice is fading; she's nearly asleep. "You know, what happens next?"

"Nothing," Wayne whispers. "If we're really lucky, nothing at all."